JAY, JAKE
AND JIMMY

First Edition

Published by The Nazca Plains Corporation
Las Vegas, Nevada
2009

ISBN: 978-1-935509-65-3

Published by

The Nazca Plains Corporation ®
4640 Paradise Rd, Suite 141
Las Vegas NV 89109-8000

PUBLISHER'S NOTE
Jay, Jake and Jimmy is a work of fiction created wholly by *Wade
Wright's* imagination. All characters are fictional and any resemblance
to any persons living or deceased is purely by accident. No portion of
this book reflects any real person or events.

Cover Photos,
Les Byerley and Andrey Vishnyakov

Art Director,
Blake Stephens

Acknowledgement & Dedication

To each and every individual that has successfully found their, 'true life of living', and if you are reading this book, that does include you! Welcome aboard to the life of peaceful living, and enjoying the true living of life!

JAY, JAKE
AND JIMMY

First Edition

Wade Wright

Contents

Chapter 1

Who's Who

City Gym sounds more like a boxing gym, and rightfully should! City Gym was started as a boxing only, gym about 30 years ago. But thanks to its success in its neighborhood, it has grown to a complete boxing training center, weightlifting center and swimming center, for the younger athletic individuals, on the northern side of town.

Jim Stempff, called Jimmy by all of his friends and co-workers, had just moved into the area from Cleveland and was renting an apartment about three blocks from the gym. Being a very athletic type of guy and very well built from his prior eight years of weightlifting, he had quickly inquired around, about which gym and where he should be joining to continue his working out and getting some exercise. The City Gym was "the place" according to all the others that he had asked. Some did mention another athletic club, but told him that they did not think he would like that place nearly as much as the City Gym.

Jimmy did not even bother checking out the other athletic club, once he visited the City Gym. His attitude was, this is it! It has got what I want, it's convenient and the price is right. Why bother checking out another place that others have already said that I probably would not like, as well as this place. After the "official" tour and the getting joined process, Jimmy used the pool and then hit his favorite part of any athletic club, the weightlifting room.

He had, of course, seen the weightlifting area on the tour, but was quite surprised of how many guys were in there once he got done in the pool. His membership here was already turning out to be a positive. Jimmy had gotten into the weightlifting scene, originally, only because of all of the beautiful bodies that work out in a lifting room. That was his original reason, but after making some headway on his own body, he gained more "goal oriented" reasons. He, early on, realized he was becoming one of the beautiful bodies. Today at age 26, he weighted right at 185 pounds, stood 6'1" tall, had a very short blond flat top hair cut, and a very nicely tailed strip of blond hair running down his muscular chest. His waist was about 32" and his chest was probably about a 46," so the body structure was very attractive.

After working out for about an hour, give or take another 30 minutes or so of additional time, for his paying more attention to other bodies than to his own, he headed for the locker room to shower and get ready to leave.

The locker room was actually one large room, divided into smaller sections so that a grouping of lockers and a center bench each took up about one fourth of the total space. On Jimmy's original tour, this arrangement was a little disappointing to him. His concern was that if there happened to be some really strong good looking hunk in the room, he might be in one of the other spaces and out of comfortable view. Hey he decided, 'One of the pits of life a guy has to live with, I guess.'

Jimmy stripped from his now sweaty lifting shorts and T-shirt, grabbed the towel that so proudly said "City Gym" on it and headed for the shower room. Jimmy had realized years ago that a busy shower room always takes longer to have a shower in, than an empty one. Laughing to himself, he always pondered that situation and just wondered why. He always figured – I'm not any dirtier when the shower room is crowded, than I am when it is empty. Observations and drooling he decided – takes time.

Just as Jimmy had almost completely dried off, had his pants and shoes on, and was just ready to pull his T-shirt on, a "new" visitor to the locker room showed up. Having his key in hand for a locker, Jimmy prayed that the correct locker would be in his bench section.

BONGO! Luck! As the "new" man checked his key number against the number on the door, he apologized to Jimmy for being so close and rather forcing Jimmy to move a little to the right so the man could sit down.

"Why do they always seem to give a guy coming in, a locker that is right beside a guy getting ready to leave," the new man asked. "I always find it so funny that with all of the space available, that almost always happens. I'm really sorry for kind of squeezing in here."

"Hey no bother at all," Jimmy responded. "Yeah, it is funny that two guys end up right beside each other when there are all of the other spaces available. But, I guess the guy giving out the keys don't know when a guy is getting ready to leave, does he?"

"No, I guess not, but I will say that I have tried to figure out in the past if there is actually some way for him to know. It just happens so often, it makes you wonder if maybe they have a hidden TV in here that they can check before they give you a key. Hey – maybe they do! Maybe that is their way of getting guys to know each other. What do you think?"

"Well, I don't see any cameras anyplace, but you know they have them so damn small now that a guy can wear one as a shirt button, so I guess anything is possible. But if your idea is correct, I'm Jim Stempff, but everybody calls me Jimmy." Jimmy held his hand out for a handshake, but had to pause for a moment since the "new man" was busy removing his trousers.

"Oh, I'm sorry!" The newcomer replied as he held out his hand to shake hands with Jimmy. "I'm Jake Oasley. Glad to meet you!"

"Yeah, I'm glad to meet you too. I saw where your gym bag has the "J. Oasley" on the side of it, but I of course did not know what the "J" stood for."

"Well, it stands for Jake. But I've never really cared for the name Jake, so I just let it go as 'J'."

"Oh, OK! Then calling you just 'J' is OK? I can almost do more than guess, that you are headed for the weight room right?"

"Yeah, I try to get in at least a couple of workouts a week. When I'm out of town it really makes it rough to do though. I would assume from looking at you, that you use the weight room too, right?"

"Yeah, I do, but looking at you, obviously not as regularly as you do. I'm glad you came in before I got out of here. Maybe we can workout sometime together, if that is OK with you. I'm new around here, just moved from Cleveland and today is my first day here."

"Jimmy, I will be much more than glad to work out with you, but I have to tell you I never know more than about an hour ahead of time of when I will be able to get here. I have very little self-control over my work schedule. So I'm really sorry I can't agree on a specific time. If I did, I would be letting you down, and I simply will not do that. Understand? I will workout with you whenever we can make it happen though! OK?"

"Sure 'J', I understand." Jimmy replied as he watched the big strong muscle man pull on his shorts, and pull down the hem of his tank top. Jimmy had fumbled and stumbled, and had taken up about as much time as he could getting himself ready to leave. All of a sudden he decided the smaller dressing areas were a plus, rather than a negative.

As he gathered his gym bag and towel together to leave, he stepped over the bench, patted 'J' on the shoulder and rather promised him that he would see him later. He managed to take one more lingering look at the, 6 foot one or two, 210 to 215 pound, muscle, solid, solid muscle, black man, before he had to finally leave the room. The man had the chest of death on him, a waist line that any teen aged dancer would be jealous of, and of course legs that could hold up the main structure of a bridge across the Mississippi! Shear solid steel! Every bit of him – the neck – the chest – the arms – the back – the legs – the whole freaking body! Jimmy could, of course, only guess about his age, as he had about his other measurements, but he guessed him to be probably about 31 or 32 years old. He thought, hey, with the looks that he's got, he could be a lot older and just look that young. 'Maybe – maybe, someday I will get to find out. And maybe someday I will get to find out for sure why he did not have a wedding ring on. Does he not have a wedding ring, or does he take it off when he comes to workout?'

Having the situation of being right beside 'J' on the bench, Jimmy did get a chance, not as long of a chance as he really wanted, but none the less, a chance to see 'J's dick before he got his workout shorts on. About all Jimmy could think about, right at that time was, he had better put on something longer than shorts, if he is going to keep that inside. That dick looked as strong and as muscled as all of the rest of the bronze statue of a man that he was so close to! The whole sight of the man was so great, that Jimmy even took in big deep breaths of air, just hoping to get a slight sniff of the scent of any part of his magnificent hunk of a man!

Jimmy wanted to, without any explanation, simply reach out and grab onto any part of the body that he could, or even better, lick any part of skin that he could get to! And just seeing what was there and so close, he knew just what part of the body he'd like to lick first!

Jimmy had always been rather, maybe a little more than just jealous of black men and their ability to; #1 always seem to have a large dick between their legs, and #2, their ability to really make the weight room work for them. 'J' had shown both of the positives. He was carrying the type of dick that Jimmy has always had the most fun with, whenever he could get one like that to play with. And all of those muscles on that body, were definitely enough to make even some old, frail, can't hardly see, half dead, straight man – get all excited. All this man needed to do to shake people up was to put on a tight sleeveless T-shirt, and walk down the street! Hot, hot, hot!!!

A walking piece of museum artwork!

Jimmy returned to his apartment feeling glad that he had worked out, but at the same time really wishing that he had not started to dress out quite so soon so that he could have stayed in the weight room longer and admired that magnificent sculptured body. His not knowing just when, or even if they ever would be working out together, really bothered Jimmy. There was so much more about 'J' that Jimmy was just so hungry to find out.

What type of work does 'J' do – that is so controlling? Where does he live? What does he drive? What time of the day does he normally get to work out? Is he married, single, gay? Is there somebody else in his life? How old is he really? How big does that stick get when it gets hard? IF –big 'IF,' – he is gay – is he a top or a bottom? And even if he's not gay, does he let the guys in the shower room look at his rod, and heaven for bid, does he ever let other guys touch it and feel how strong it is?

'Damn!' Jimmy thought, 'He did not do one damn thing today that would give me any indication that maybe he is gay. He acted so damn straight! When his dick was out, he did not act like he wanted me to see it or anything. Damn, I'll bet he is straight and probably has a whole bunch of kids – since – if, I was his wife, I'd be wanting sex with him every night! Maybe he is straight, and I'm just praying that he is gay. Maybe he is gay, and I'm not his type. Maybe that is the really "Why" he can't commit to working out with me. Maybe he was just being really nice and wishing I would hurry up and leave! Maybe I'm not big enough and muscular enough for him. Maybe he has a lover. Oh, Shit! If he does! Oh God! How I would love to be that puppy for just a little while! At least while in bed!!!!! Oh the idea of getting that dick all hard and rammed up in my ass, as well as getting to play with all of that muscle mass is way too much for me to even think about.'

'Hey I just hope I get a chance to know the guy, even if I do have to realize that some woman is the one that gets to take him to the hay stack each night!'

Jimmy attempted to get his new life kind of organized without pondering the 'J' too much. The whole sight of that guy, and the mental image of him just made Jimmy want to find him again.

Although Jimmy had been to the gym three times during this past week, he never saw 'J'.

That is until one day while driving into a convenience store parking lot, and 'J' was driving out. 'J' did not see Jimmy, he assumed. Well, so he hoped since 'J' did not make any type of reaction that he had seen or noticed Jimmy. When he waved to 'J' he thought 'J' had seen it, but then he had to decide that he had not. Or – the big bad 'OR' – 'J' really was not interested in getting to know Jimmy, and purposely did avoid waving to him. And of course maybe, just maybe 'J' was not nearly as excited in meeting Jimmy as the reverse was, and 'J' simply did not remember meeting him.

Jimmy felt rather disappointed that he had come so close to getting to talk to 'J' again, and have it not quite happen. One good thought was – 'J' did not have a wife and a bunch of kids in the car anyway! That was a 'goodie' for him.

Another week went by and finally, on that Friday afternoon, Jimmy just happened to go to the locker room and 'J' was picking up his gym bag and towel. Very similar situation as the last time, but reversed positions this time. 'J' was fully clothed and was started toward the door as Jimmy was looking for his locker number.

Jimmy quickly stopped and said, "Hi, 'J', how are you today?"

'J' turned, and said, "Uh – Hi, how are you?"

Jimmy immediately got the concept that 'J' certainly was in no way as excited about knowing Jimmy as Jimmy was in knowing 'J'.

Jimmy just asked, "How have you been?" and 'J' replied, "OK man, how are you doing?"

Jimmy could easily tell 'J' was not interested in hanging around talking, so he quickly told him, "Oh, I'm doing OK. Glad to see you, take care!"

'J' responded, "OK man, you take care, OK?" and then left the room.

Jimmy very quickly decided that his dreaming of ever getting to even know 'J' very well was not a good probability, and he also decided that the heavenly ideas of ever being in bed with him – if he is gay, certainly were not going to be a possibility!

He dressed into his workout clothes, did his work out, showered, dressed and left the gym. He was feeling so down, he did not even make any attempts to try and talk to any of the other guys working out that day. He truly felt depressed!

After that rather "brush off" encounter, Jimmy had really decided that he wished now, that he had never met 'J' in the first place. He did not care for this feeling of being put down and put out.

Each time that Jimmy went to the gym he was actually glad that he did not run into 'J' again, since being around that guy was just way too exciting to him, for not being able to be really close to him.

For a month, that worked. Then one Saturday afternoon, a day of the week when Jimmy did not usually use for going to the gym, he felt that he needed a workout and did go to the gym, only to find 'J' in the weight room.

As he entered the room, he of course spotted 'J'. 'J' just is not a person that you can miss when you are in the same room with him.

'J' saw Jimmy enter the room, and although Jimmy decided to kind of stay on the opposite side and do some squats over there, 'J' came over and said, "Hi," as soon as he got done doing his bench presses.

"Hi! How you doing? I've been watching for you, but I guess our timing has not worked. I'm really sorry, but I can't remember your name."

"Uh, Hi. I'm Jimmy, how you doing?" Jimmy was feeling really confused, but nonetheless, glad that 'J' had come over to greet him.

"Doing OK, but sure have been busy and out of town a lot, so I'm sure that has helped keeping us out of the gym at the same time. How you doing getting settled in town?"

"I'm doing OK. Kind of have my apartment all in shape now, and getting to know where stuff is around here. I saw you a couple of weeks after we met, but I guess you didn't know who I was."

"You did? Where were we? What – I didn't say 'Hi' to you, or something?"

"Yeah, you were pulling out of that convenience store down the street from here, and I was pulling in and waved. You just kind of looked my direction and then drove off. Then there was that one day when you were leaving here just as I came in."

"Jimmy, I am really sorry! I don't remember either of those times! My mind has really been swimming with troubles at work and with customers. I guess I have not been acting very sharp. I'm really sorry! I know I was supposed to be over at Mom's house one night, and I completely forgot about that! My ass got in trouble with her over that one! So anyway Jimmy, I am really, really very sorry that I was not acknowledging you when I should have been. Can you forgive me?"

"Yeah, I'm just feeling better now knowing that you really don't dislike me as much as I had thought you did."

"Oh shit, Jimmy, I am so damn sorry! I will have to make that up to you someday, some way. I really feel like shit right now."

"Hey 'J', don't worry about it. I'm just glad we are kind of back talking to each other. I have to admit that I had been avoiding this place for a while since I really did not want to run into you. I had no idea you would be here today, or I would not have come today, either."

The renewed friendship lifters spend the better part of an hour and a half working out together. 'J' gave Jimmy some good pointers on how to maximize his working out to gain as much bulk as possible. But he did point out the ole standard – "No pain – no gain!!!"

Of course with that statement, Jimmy could not help but think of his ass and how he would love to feel the gain and pain back there. A steel rod, yeah, but not the type that holds weights.

Still, 'J' had given no indication of his sexuality. No comments, no actions, no-nothing, that Jimmy could attempt to read to figure 'J' out. Jimmy just felt that if he knew for sure, even if 'J' is straight, knowing that would be so much better than his constant hoping.

Following the workout, the men headed for the shower room and the good, cool, refreshing shower. Jimmy would have forgone all of the lifting and working out today, if that had been necessary, just to get to the shower room with 'J'.

Jimmy attempted to act as if he was not looking, but he had to wonder, quite often, if 'J' was catching him admire that steak hanging from the front of himself. He did!

When the shower room finally emptied, except for the two of them, 'J' then leaned over toward Jimmy, smiled a very big grin, ran his eyes up and down Jimmy's body, and asked, "Hey man, do you happen to know of any way that I can make up to you for me not realizing who you were, when you waved, and then also the time we saw each other in here?"

The very quiet, gentle, and soft way that 'J' had asked the question, as well as they way 'J' had openly admired the entire length of Jimmy's body, made Jimmy very suddenly, and immediately, look up at 'J' in complete shock. "Oh shit man! Are you asking what I think you are?"

"Could be! All depends on you. I could take you over to the ice cream shop and buy you a sundae, to make up for my goof-ups, or I could offer you a steak dinner, which would be served at my house! Which do you think you might like to get? Which do you think you might enjoy the most? Which turns your buttons on the most?"

"Forget the ice cream sundae! Oh my God, 'J' is this for real? Do you really mean it?"

Jimmy then leaned much closer to 'J' and very quietly asked him, "Are you offering sex to me? That is what you mean, isn't it?"

Looking at Jimmy's face, with the smile and wide grin on it, 'J' knew his question had hit the spot. "Hell yes, man! If you want it. I think you are really cute and well built, and if you like it up the butt, I think I could make up for my goof-ups to you that way! What do you think man?"

"You mean now? You mean we can go do it now? Oh hell yes 'J' – I'm sure ready!"

Jimmy had to consciously keep his voice down. He had gotten so excited that he was afraid the other guys in the locker room would be able to hear him. "Let's go man. Oh 'J', please don't make this be a joke, OK?"

"No joke, man. Let's go!"

The men quickly exited the shower room and went into the locker room. Jimmy's locker was the closer one, and was in a different grouping than 'J's' was. He headed for his dressing area and 'J' continued on to the next area.

All of a sudden Jimmy heard somebody say, "Hey Jake, I didn't know you were going to be working out today!"

Then he heard 'J' reply with, "Hey Jay, I did not know you were going to be here either." Then in a lower volume, he heard 'J' say, "Hey Bro. I and Jimmy are going over to the house. Do you want to join us, or workout?" Then in an even lower voice Jimmy heard him continue, "If you go with us, I know you will be getting a good workout there too."

Without even knowing who 'J' was taking to, that last statement really turned Jimmy on. He figured, any guy that 'J' invited along had to be OK. Then he realized he had heard him refer to him as Bro. But, was that just a friendship thing, or was it really his brother?

"Who is Jimmy? Have I met him before? I don't know who that is."

"Stick your head around the corner, he's the cute white guy getting dressed. He's the only one over there."

As Jay poked his head around the corner of the lockers, he swung his head back around toward 'J' and told him, "Jake, that is the same guy that I told you about a few weeks ago that I wanted to play with, but screwed it up because I left too early. He's the guy that I told you I think I could have gotten, if I had talked to him some."

Jimmy had heard the comments, and had also seen Jay, as he poked his head around the corner. Still without any clothing on at all, Jimmy came running around the bank of lockers.

"Oh my God!! Oh my God!" Jimmy exclaimed over and over! You two are identical twins! You are identical twins! Which one is which?"

Well, that question would not have been necessary if Jimmy would have checked things out a little more closely. Both men were naked. Jake had not yet started to get dressed, and Jay was just to the point of putting his jock strap on when Jake came around the corner. Identical, yes – well almost, yes. Both men had obviously been working out in the weight room together and keeping their bulking up pretty well equal, but regardless of how hard a man tries, it has never been a reality of actually being able to enlarge a cock, even one or two inches in length. Jay's beefsteak was longer! Yes, it was a little longer, but still longer than 99 and 44% of the men walking the streets on any day!

"Oh God! Is Jay the one that I thought was you, that day, in here?" Jimmy asked. Is he the one that drives the red convertible?"

"Guess you are right man. The day that you two kind of talked in here, he came home and was pissed that he had kind of let a possible, possibility go by, by not hanging around in here to get to talk to you. He was pissed because he really liked what he saw, and he wanted to get to your ass. Still interested on going to the house?"

"Hell yes man. Shit, I'm more anxious now than before and I'm ready!"

"And yeah, he has a red convertible. The day he came home all pissed at himself, I didn't know it was you he was talking about!"

"So you have been thinking that I was not talking to you, and it was really him that you had seen! Oh shit man, I'm glad we have this little mess straightened up! I really do think it is time that we get something straight between us, don't you?"

"Hell yes, I do! And damn quick!" Jimmy stated.

Of course Jay decided to join the other two rather than stay at the gym. He said that was a no-brainer! All three men dressed, and Jimmy, for some rather unknown reason, was the first to get completely dressed and ready to go.

As they went to the parking lot, Jake said, "Well, since we each have a car here, I guess we will create a parade going to the house. I will take the lead, and Jay, you follow Jimmy so that he does not change his mind about this, part way there, and cut down some side street to get away. OK?"

Jimmy's immediate response, "Hell men, I'm the one that is afraid that you two might change your minds. If there is any possibility of that, I'll spread them right here in the parking lot so that you can both do me here on the asphalt, and I won't care who is watching."

"Whoa, whoa, Jimmy!" Jay said. "Don't talk like that in front of me. That gets me too excited and I just might throw you down right here and now, if you get me any more excited!"

Jake told Jimmy that Jay's idea of living, is to live in the nude, and do anything you wish, anyplace you wish. They have had some problems in the past of trying to keep his pants on him when necessary, so the whole family is careful now not to mention anything that could get him all excited at the wrong place.

"The family used to think it was funny for him to take off all of his clothes, and run around naked, when he was a little boy. Well, he never out grew it! Now the family wishes that they had made him stay in the house when he was naked."

"Oh, shit man!" Jay interjected. "It just plain feels good to let it all hang out, and damn it, everybody knows how the human body is built, so why not let it go free?"

"Uh – Jay!" Jimmy replied. "I kind of think you are really wrong about how everybody knows how the human body is built. Jay, you are not built like the normal human body man! No way in hell man! I saw it in the locker room. I've had a lot of stuff rammed up in my ass before, and some of it not so small, but shit man, right now I am standing here, kind of shaking and nervous, thinking that you are going to be ramming that hunk of meat of yours up in me! I'm sure I know why you like to be naked. For your entire life people have looked at you, and made you a special person because of what you are hanging down there. Well anyway, those that have had the pleasure of seeing it!"

"Which brings me to another question. And to me, it's kind of an important, but exciting, question. Do both of you guys have dicks that get really hard and stiff?"

As Jake and Jay both agreed that, yes, they do get hard and stiff, Jimmy only stood there and kind of shuttered. The thought of either one of those dicks going up in his asshole was kind of scary to Jimmy. But he continued to smile! The mere thought of either one of those beautiful big thick sticks of meat, going up inside of him, made him smile and shutter, all at the same time!

Jimmy had gotten all confused about what to call each of the men, since it seemed like both of them went by 'J' or Jay, which could not be distinguished apart when spoken.

Jake told Jimmy, "OK, now that the two of us are together, you call me Jake and we will call him Jay. When I originally told you to call me 'J', I had no idea at that time that you would be together with both of us at the same time. If I had thought you were one of the playful types, then I might have thought it was possible, but I really figured you would probably have PTA meetings on the brain. Wrong, I guess!"

"Yeah, you are wrong about that. Probably the reason I came across so straight the first time was that I was so damn afraid that every bit of gay I had in me was showing. As soon as I saw you, I praised the Lord that I had left Cleveland! Then I was just damn afraid that I might have been wrong, or that at least, my hopes were all wrong. Now Damn! I'm not only right, I'm double right! Oh God! I cannot imagine this is really me with the two of you. Man, I want to be the middleman today. Can I be in the middle?"

"Come on men, we need to get to your house!"

Chapter 2

Whose T-Shirt Is This, Anyway?

With Jake in the lead, Jimmy in the middle, and Jay following, Jimmy realized that even during the drive to the house, he had been put in exactly the spot that he was looking so forward to. In the middle! Even this driving situation was exciting to Jimmy. He was allowing his mind to expand on his excitement of "being in the middle," although they were not even yet to the house. Jimmy was really starting to get himself all, really, excited about the soon to be, "being the middle," without the cars being involved.

As Jay turned into a driveway, Jimmy parked his car along the street curb realizing that Jay would probably need to park his, now rather infamous – at least between the three of them – red convertible beside Jake's car in the driveway.

All three men approached the side door of the house at, about, the same time. As Jake unlocked the side door and opened it, Jay moved up close behind Jimmy and grabbed his ass. "Hey, this feels damn right good to me, brother. I think we found ourselves one nice, tight, little, ass to play with. Shit man, I can't wait to get him inside and get him good and naked, like all men are supposed to be. My dick is feeling kind of lonely right now, and it needs a good warm spot to hide in. Jimmy, do you think maybe your ass will warm up my little dickie some?"

"Shit man," Jimmy replied. "I sure as the hell know that my little tight ass, as you call it, is more than ready to give your dick someplace to get all warm, and cozy, but if I was you, I certainly would not be calling your dick, some 'little dickie'. There sure as hell is nothing little about that side of beef that you're carrying there, man!"

As they entered the house, Jimmy turned to his two, new, hot, hunky, muscular, hung stud friends and rather asked, to either one, but to neither one in particular, "Do you both live here?"

Jake told Jimmy, "Yeah, man. This used to be the family home, but since Mom is now living with her sister, Jay and I use this place. Since I'm out of town so much, Jay kind of gets it all to himself, most of the time. Well – I should say – all to himself and whoever his playmate of the day is. Whenever I get home, from an out of town trip, I always find some new clothes lying around someplace, that I just know damn well are not Jay's. Some guy his size is not going to be wearing a size small shirt or a size 28" briefs. I mean, it's OK with me. He can play around with whoever he wants, but damn I just wish that when they tear off their clothes all over the house, that they would remember where they threw them so that they could go back and pick 'em up. I come home to a house that looks like maybe it's been a gay bathhouse for a week or so. The shirts and that kind of stuff I can understand, but the day I found the 28" briefs laying in the front hallway, really made me wonder. Really wondered if I'd find some guy's pants around here, too. Never did, so I guess he didn't leave here naked. 28" waist! I've always kind of wished that one would come back while I'm here. I want to see that small little fucker! I really want to know just how Jay used him!"

"Oh sit, man!" Jay jokingly snapped back to Jake, "The only reason that I don't get to see just what you leave lying around is because whatever the hotel maid can pick up, she does. And for the guys that you just leave lying around when you leave, then the maids just chase them away. I'll bet you get a whole lot more fucking and sucking while you are out of town, than I do staying here. Hey, when you are traveling, you are always the "new meat" in town, and all types are trying to get into your silkies!"

"You ass! I do not wear silkies! And you know very damn well I don't! Thank goodness Jimmy has already seen me dress out in the gym or with that statement he could have decided that maybe he had gone home with the wrong two guys."

As Jake closed some blinds on some of the more obvious front windows, he turned to Jimmy and explained. "I usually try to remember to close these when Jay is here and especially when we have somebody else in the house with us. Remember I told you how he loves to run around naked, and he does not care who sees him. I'll tell you, I really wonder just what kind of a show goes on here when I am not home. I came home Wednesday and one of the younger guys from down the street saw me at the grocery store and asked me if that was me at the house the night before. I told him, 'no, I was out of town'. Then he just kind of acted like he wanted to change the subject and just said, 'Ohhh'. When I asked him why, he acted like he really was sorry he had mentioned it. I'll bet he saw Jay running around in here, nude."

"Is that guy gay?" Jimmy asked.

"Well, I don't know. But I want to. Maybe I should have told him that it was me, just to see what he said. I do know I am certainly going to be paying more attention to him from now on though, to try and find out. I've been noticing him and his tight little ass for about three years now and if there is a possibility, I want to punch it. Either I find out, or I will make sure Jay finds out for me. I want a piece of that ass if at all possible! Hell – maybe that size small shirt I found is his! Jay! Jay! Is that shirt I found in the hall bath, Patrick's – from down the street?"

As Jay came back down the hall from the bedroom area, he was already naked. Jimmy took one very deep strong breath as he got a good long look at Jay's muscular naked body and his, 'front cover of a muscle mag,' presence of a man. One hell of a big strong, muscular, handsome man, and his big strong, thick, meaty, seven inch, hanging steak. His mind went completely bonkers as he realized that Jay did not even have the start of a hard-on yet. "Oh shit!" He thought. "Oh my god! That thing will be getting bigger when it gets hard. Oh shit men, let's get with it. Man, I really need it, and I'm getting way too anxious to try and act like, 'no big deal'."

"What man?" Jay asked Jake as he entered the living room. "What you want man?"

"Hey, that size small T-shirt that I found in the bathroom the other day – is that by any chance Patrick's, from down the street? Is that where it came from?"

"Well, why do you want to know, man? What difference does it make whose shirt it is?"

"When you find a shirt laying around that obviously does not belong in this house, you kind of wonder if somebody went home bare-chested, or what did he wear home? Since Patrick is a small, the shirt is a small, and he could have gone home bare-chested if he happened to be here during the day, I just got to wondering if that just happened to be his. Well, bro?" Jake asked as he kind of lowered his head and looked at Jay from the top of his eyes. "Is it?"

"Yeah – man, yes it is! Yeah, he forgot it the other day when he left. I'll get it back to him."

"Jay!" Jake excitedly exclaimed. "Man when did this get started? How long have you been doing him? Jay, fill me in! Damn man, I'm getting all excited. Shit man I've had my eyes on his tight little ass ever since he came home from college, what two, three years ago? How in the hell did you and he start doing it and how long have you been fucking him?"

"Hey man, he made me promise that I would not tell anybody! Shit man! He said that he needed to keep it a secret!"

"Keep what a secret? You playing around? Is that what you mean?"

"Yeah! – Ah – Jake – you do know he is supposed to get married in November, don't you?"

"Oh shit man! Hell no! I did not know that! He is getting married and is fucking around with you too? How often have you two been getting it on? How long has this been going on?'

"Well, we started last summer. We've been doing it for about a year now. One day I had my gym trunks on while outside cutting the grass and he stopped to talk. While we were talking I offered him a beer. We came inside to get the beers, and things kind of got out of hand then."

Jake turned and kind of looked at Jimmy like, "Hey man, I know you are here, I have not forgotten about you, but man I need to find out stuff here."

Jimmy returned the look and without saying any actual words, let Jake know that everything was all OK with him. He rather made a hand signal that indicated, "All's OK man, don't worry about me, I need to hear this!"

"What do you mean things kind of got out of hand then? What happened?"

"Well, when I got the beer out, I guess I must have been feeling a little rambunctious, I guess because of some of our outside conversation, and I put the cold beer on his stomach instead of handing it to him. That kind of got us to playing around. We were just kind of goofing, you know the kind that eventually ends up in a grabbing session with someone you want to grab, but don't know if you should, or can or not?"

"Yeah – what had been said outside, that made you feeling kind of rambunctious? What had you guys been talking about that was getting you all turned on?"

"Well, he told me that he had noticed that one of us, but he did not know which one, is not real particular about closing the blinds at night. He told me that he has noticed for some time that one of us likes to run around naked, but he didn't know which one it was. When he told me that, I didn't think he was coming on to me. I thought we were just having a neighbor to neighbor conversation. But I guess the idea that he had seen me more than once, and did not complain about it, kind of got me feeling good. So when we came inside, that's when I started feeling kind of playful."

"So what happened. How and what went on?"

"Well, when I put that cold beer can on his stomach, he jumped and kind of made a squeal. Then I kind of accused him of liking it, and then he asked, I think in a joking way, 'Like what?' And of course with that, I then proceeded to show him what I thought he might like. Hey Jake, don't you remember that time you got home from out of town and there were two open, but untouched, beers on the table and you asked my why. I made up some lame excuse about why they were there. That is the time this happened. We never got back to the beers. We started goofing around and put the beers down, and then really got into it. After we kind of got tired of trying to act like, 'Oh this is no big deal, this is the way guys play all of the time,' we finally started really playing with each other."

"I still was not too sure if I was overstepping the line or not, but I kept grabbing his leg and kept getting closer and closer to his crotch and his butt, and he never said to stop. Finally, I grabbed his ass and squeezed it. He never complained, so I squeezed it tighter and tighter. He finally said, "Oh shit man, that feels so good!"

"What was he wearing? You had gym shorts on, what did he have on?'

"Well, when he came back, he had shorts on too. Not as short as mine, but kind of thin, silky type of shorts. The kind of fabric that clings to your skin. They hugged his ass and his basket really nice! I found out he did not have any jock strap on under them, either."

"What do you mean, when he came back? Back from where?"

"When he stropped to talk, that was not the first time that he had been down the street that day. He did not know it, but I did see him earlier, like about 15 minutes earlier go past the house. He had on jeans then. But when he came back and stopped to talk, he had these sexy shorts on. I think that was one of the reasons I got rambunctious and thinking playful. He had changed into shorts on purpose. I never told him that I had seen him go down the street earlier, though."

"OK, so you grabbed his ass. Then what happened?"

"Well, he kind of wilted into my arms, and kept telling me how good that felt. Shit man! I was squeezing it for all my might. I'm not so sure it was supposed to feel 'good', maybe a little more painful, but he just wilted into me. At one point I actually had to kind of hold him up so that his legs did not completely collapse. When that happened, he grabbed ahold of my left arm and squeezed it, but very lovingly. Then he laid his face over on it. When he did that, he kind of lowly asked me to please keep squeezing. So I did. He had his face kind of buried on my arm, slinking down on my chest and I had my right arm stretched around him kind of holding him up and at the same time squeezing his butt with my right hand. I felt like we were making love standing there, that way. It made my dick get hard. When that happened, Patrick leaned into it and rubbed his body against it. Of course you know damn well that made it that much harder."

"Kind of lying there on me, even though we were really kind of still standing, he had his face on my arm and he had his left arm up on my right shoulder. He then kind of slowly started lowering his left hand and moved it down along the middle of my chest. I could tell he was breathing real heavy. You know how you can, for some funny reason, know when some guy is doing something for his very first time, and he is really nervous about doing it? You know he wants to, but he is really, really nervous! Well, that is what was happening then. I could tell that he had never held another man like this, and he had never been held like this, by another man. I knew right then that I was his first gay experience. I knew that I was the first one to get to him, although he was – as I found out later, 23 years old. He kind of just kept softly asking me to please don't let go, and he kept moving his hand down lower and lower on my body. He kept taking really deep, deep breaths. I could feel his whole body rise and fall each time he took a breath."

"By this time my dick had gotten really hard. It was pushing it up against his body, and he was pushing back against it. I could tell that he had a very stiff dick. His was really hard, too. Every time I kind of pushed up against him, I could feel him pushing back, and I could tell he was making sure that it was his dick that he was pushing with. He was really rubbing that thing up against me. That was the first time that he had ever pushed his dick up against some other guy, and he was really excited doing it."

"I just knew that he was trying to get up enough nerve to reach down and touch mine. I knew that, with what we were experiencing together, right then, he should have known, that he did not have any reasons to have any fears about touching my cock. He should have known that nobody was going to slap him down for doing that! But, I just knew that as nervous and as afraid as he was, he was still having to force himself, to even think about doing that, and believing that doing it would be OK. He had never touched another man's cock before, and he had never had another man touch his cock before either, and he was really afraid. He was shaking. He was breathing real heavy. He was taking deep breaths. I could feel him quivering. His heart was pounding really hard! I could feel it pounding inside of him, from him being up against me."

"I grabbed ahold of him with my left hand, so that he was steady, and then I lowered my head down toward his ear and told him to, 'Go ahead'. He really, very quietly, asked what I meant when I said to 'Go ahead'. I told him that I wanted him to grab my cock, and that I knew he was wanting to do that. I told him that I knew how nervous he was right then, but that I wanted him to do it, and I wanted to be the guy that he gets to experience this with, for his first time. I told him that I wanted him to grab my cock as much as he wanted to do it. I told him, real gently, 'Patrick I really want to feel your hand on my dick.' I said, 'Patrick, nothing bad is going to happen to you, just because you grab and feel my dick'. Then I kind of pleaded with him, 'Patrick, please, please!' When I said that, I think he almost cried. He got kind of all weepy and said, 'Oh man can I? Can I do that?' and with that he almost just collapsed in my arms. He lowered his hand on down the front of me and got to the top of my gym shorts. He just slightly slid the tips of his fingers in under the top of my shorts. He stopped there. He was breathing real heavily! He acted like if he went any farther, that it was like illegal or something. I felt him take a very deep breath. I whispered to him, 'Do it man. I'm waiting! I want to feel your hand. I want your hand around my cock.' I grabbed ahold of him and held him real tight, so that he knew everything was OK. I bent down a little and gave the side of his neck a small kiss. Then I told him, 'Please man, I want you to do this for me!'"

"He pushed his hand down, on into my shorts and once again I thought he was going to cry. I put my hand on top of his, from the outside of my shorts, and guided it to my dick and balls and squeezed it, so that his hand would be grabbing ahold of my stuff. With my hand on top of his, we squeezed my dick. Then I moved his hand down farther and we squeezed my balls. It was kind of like I was showing him how to do it. He was so kind of freaked out by what he was actually doing, that he needed to have me help him so that he did not back out of doing it, at the last second."

"When Patrick did that, I think he had a complete life-long change. I think he had finally made a move, that he had been wanting to do for a long, long time. He was kind of going through some mental emotions like, everything he had ever been told during life, everything that was a complete 'no-no', had just now become the most exciting and pleasant experience, that he had ever lived through. In-fact, he later told me about how he had been wanting to be with me, or with you, for a long time. He told me that he had figured out, some time earlier, that we were gay, and when he realized that, that was when he started getting him all excited and anxious about doing something like this, but it had to be with one of us. He told me that he did not care which one it was, he wanted to do this with – either one of us. He told me that before that time, he had never had any apparent interest in any other guys, but when he started thinking about being in bed with one of us, it really started getting him all excited. He said that is when he started watching for us a lot more often than he ever had before. He said that he started keeping an eye on us and was really trying to just "happen to be in the right place at the right time." He finally told me later, one day while we were playing and talking, that he had gone out purposely, and bought those silky, thin, sexy, shorts that he had on that day, just to have them on sometime when he got the chance to talk to one of us."

"What? He told you that he had been wanting to be with you or me? Shit man! Damn, I wish I had known that! Shit man, I've been wanting to pound that little ass of his for years now!" Jake proclaimed!

"So what happened after he got ahold of you? What went on then?"

"We just stood there for what seemed like a long time. Probably not that long, but for what we both were experiencing right then, it did seem like a long time. He continued to hug me and continued to rub my dick. Finally, I kind of moved him to the side a little and I reached down and started sliding my shorts down. When I did that, I felt him take real deep breaths again. I kind of think every different action right then was another very nervous 'first' for him. There were so many times that I just thought he could just sit down and cry. I think what was happening, or I should say, finally happening, was such a great experience for him, to finally be doing it, that it was really getting to him emotionally. I guess he had dreamed of this day for a long time, and it took a lot of guts and a lot of pre-planning for him to finally get it done."

"He finally pushed my shorts down far enough that my cock flipped out. He almost yelled, 'Oh Shit,' when it came out. Then he said, 'Oh My God! Oh God! How long I have been wanting to see this!' He was acting like it was something really very unusual. It was just a dick, for gosh sakes!"

"Hey Jay," Jimmy said. "To you – that might be just a normal dick! But shit man – to even me – it is an enormous hunk of meat, and for some guy that has never had another man's dick in his hands before, I can be sure he wanted to cry. What a dick to start some guy out on! So what did you two do then? Shit man, this is great! I wish I had been that Patrick guy!"

"He told me that he had seen me through the window before, naked of course, but he was never sure which one of us it was. He told me that when he came back to talk that first day, if anything could happen, he did not care which one of us it was. He had decided that the day had come for him to finally 'do it'! He did come back looking for some sex action, and he finally got it!"

"Well," Jake asked, "What action did he get that day? And how many more days have there been, since then?"

"Oh, that first day he did not get as much action as he has learned to take since then. Sir, Jake – I will have to admit that Patrick and I have been very glad, oh – for about the last year, every time you had to go out of town. I have been conducting school sessions here, while you were gone, and my student Patrick has learned a lot during that time. He's moved a long way from being afraid of grabbing my dick!"

"That first day he was so damn nervous and scared, that about all that happened, was for us to eventually go to the bedroom and lay down on the bed together for quite some time. I knew that I was going to have to take it at his pace, or I would scare him away. That first day he basically just played with my body, rubbing it and being up close to it, licking it, kind of biting on my tits some, and of course rubbing my dick. A couple of times he just asked if he could just lay on top of me and let our naked bodies touch and slide on each other. One time he did ask me to just lay on top of him, while he laid on his stomach. He did make me promise, though, that I would not try to do anything with his ass. You know, while we were lying there, that way, I do kind of think he was imagining what it might feel like to have a guy lying on him, while that guy is fucking his ass. At that time he sure wasn't ready for the fucking part, but I do think he had it on his mind, when he had me on top of him. I think that's why he wanted to feel me on top of him, that way. He wanted to know what it will feel like, to have a man on top of him, as he is getting his ass fucked. He wanted to know the feeling of the man's body up there. He just was not ready for the, 'getting it in the ass', part yet."

"That whole time he just kept saying stuff like, 'Oh, man I can't believe I'm finally doing this!' Or, stuff like, 'Oh, shit man! I have wanted to hold you for so damn long. I can't believe that I am actually doing it!' Then he would squeeze me, real tight! He did not suck me that day. He was too scared. He kept looking at it, but I knew he was way too afraid, yet, to even ask him to lick on it. The way he kept looking at it though. I knew it would not be too may sessions later, before he found out what it felt like in his mouth. When he looked at it, I kind of felt like he was worshipping it. He handled it like it would break. He had dreamed about getting ahold of one of our dick's for so long, he really did have trouble realizing that it was actually attached to me."

"We talked about him maybe putting the tip of it in his mouth, and once, he did try to lean way down close to it, and I thought then for a moment that he was going to stick it in his mouth, but then he sat up and kind of cried that he just couldn't right then. I saw his body kind of shake. I knew what his mind was going through. He was really going through some emotions that day! He was doing a lot of things that he had never thought he would be doing, and things that he thought, he should not even be thinking about doing. I told him that we would do that, let him lick my dick, later, when he was ready. But he did get his first blow job that day. He's a little guy, but for as small as he is, he's got a big dick, and he shoots big thick loads. Like probably three times that first day! Damn he was loaded and ready. He's got nice tight nuts too. Damn, I love to chew on them. And I guess he likes it too. He's pretty quick putting them in my mouth, whenever he gets a chance to."

"That first day I did not even try to get close to his asshole. That's all changed now, though! But that first day, I was afraid that he would jump up and run. But I did ask him if he was interested in fingering me some, and he said 'Yes', that he wanted to do that, if possible. While he was fingering my ass, he asked me to explain some of the types of activities that gay guys do together. I could tell which ones kind of got him all excited, and which ones did not. Of course, over the months, we have been practicing all of those that kind of turn him on. He jokes now saying stuff like, "Well we didn't do that quite right, did we teach? We will have to do that one again, right teach? I guess he likes playing the roll of being the student and me being the teacher. And of course, doing that, gives him the chance to say things like we need to do it again to try and get it right this time. Over the months, he certainly has changed his mind about what goes up in his ass. I've found out that he is a good, obedient, bottom boy!'"

Jay turned directly to Jake, and told him, "I did ask Patrick once if he thought he might like to be in bed with both of us at the same time, sometime, and he said yes. Well, actually – he looked at me and with a very big grin on his face, and he almost kind of yelled, 'Yes, Sir, I do! Oh shit man! For years now I have wanted to be in bed with one of you, whichever one I happened to get, and now you are suggesting that I could be in bed with both of you at the same time? Oh shit man, that's hot!' He admitted that he did not know for sure if that is something that he should suggest, or not, but that he would like to do that. He said that he had been fantasizing about that for a long time now. He's real anxious for that! I thought about trying to set up a session where you would "just happen" to walk in on us, while I was, maybe, fucking him, or something. I thought maybe I could work it out where it was a surprise to you and to him, at the same time."

"Well, shit man! Jake replied. "When did you ask him that? How long ago has that been?"

"Oh, shit, don't get your shorts all crammed up in your asshole brother. It was, only, about maybe two or three weeks ago. And hell, you have been gone most of that time, so don't fret. You did not miss out on any sex, man. But, brother – I think I should point out to you that, we have ourselves another hot small, sweet, tight ass standing right here between us, and we are not taking advantage of that situation, or that hole. So I do think it is time that you get him in there, get him all stripped down, show him the sling, the chains, the gags, the tit clamps, the dildos, the ropes, all the rest of the stuff, and start getting him ready! Right?"

"God, Jay! You are going to scare the hell out of him! Don't mention that stuff until we have him all undressed so that he can't bolt out the door! Thank goodness everybody doesn't run around naked like you do! Once in awhile that needs to be used as a control device, you know! Come on Jimmy, let's go to the bedroom, but don't panic about what he said. We will only be doing what you want to do today. OK?"

"Yeah, that's OK, but I will have to be real honest and truthful with you. If what Jay was mentioning back there is a reality, you guys have just found yourself another new playmate that might be kind of hard to get rid of. I have not had a chance to play with anybody that has any "equipment," since I moved, so right now I am really hoping that he was not kidding. Was he?"

"No Jimmy, he wasn't kidding! But I do have to admit to you, that I certainly would not have guessed that you were the type. Shit man, us finding each other just may turn out to be a real goody, for all of us. I know I am out of town a lot, but when I am gone, Jay will still be here and you two can do each other if you both want. Jay loves to take our really big thick, fat, dildo up his butt, but it takes somebody else to push it in for him, so I know he is going to be very happy that you are a 'complete' player. Oh, Yeah! – I forgot about Patrick. Well – maybe there will three of you all involved. Hey, when I'm home, maybe we can set up some four-ways! How's that sounding? I've got to find out from Jay, just how far he has taken Patrick into the 'equipment' part of play. I wonder if he has used any dildos on Patrick yet? Shit, if Patrick is getting fucked by Jay, which to me it sounds like maybe he is, I'm sure he is taking dildos, too. Jay made the comment about how Patrick has changed his mind about what goes up his ass. Jay probably got him started on dildos, so that he could work him up to taking something the size of Jay's stick! I can't really feature some virgin ass taking Jay's dick as his first fucking. Hell, that damn thing would make any freshman fuckee scream and run for cover! I wonder if he has gotten Patrick to ram that big dildo up in his butt for him, yet. Hell, if Patrick has become such a very obedient bottom boy, maybe Jay is running that big dildo up in his ass. My God! If a year ago Patrick had never been fucked, and now he is taking that big dildo up in his ass, Jay certainly has been a good teacher! Hey, Jimmy, it sounds like you got involved with us at a very interesting time, didn't you?"

"Jake, I kind of think that getting involved with you and Jay at <u>any</u> time, would be an interesting time! I've got one question though that I have been kind of wanting to ask."

"Yeah, what?"

"Well, you and Jay are brothers. When you guys have sex with others, do you two have sex with each other, too? Do you two ever just have sex – with just each other?"

Chapter 3

Johnny Does Some Teaching

"Yeah, and yeah." Jake answered. "When we have someone with us, that person is of course our main objective, but there are times when that 'something' happens between just the two of us, and then that just makes the play that much more meaningful for all three of us. As far as just the two of us. It's – kinda – yeah – sometimes, but not like it used to be when we were younger. You know when you are young, you really don't have too many options on finding some guy to play with, so we took advantage of having each other here, already in the house."

"Do you feel kind of weird, having sex with your own brother? I mean, since I have no brothers I have never had that chance to do something like that, but to me, I would think that the two of you doing it would seem just a little weird. Maybe not, but then, like I said, how would I know?"

"You know Jimmy, when you are a younger, it's easier to do stuff than when you are older. You don't analysis it so much. You have some crazy drive to do something, and you just do it!"

"So – so do you mind if I ask how you two got started playing with each other?"

"No, really Jimmy, I don't mind. That's because neither Jay nor I feel that anything was wrong, nor that it's anything that we need to hide. Well, from certain people, anyway! When we were young, I don't know, like maybe 16 or 17 we tried to talk the normal, guy way, about girls. You know we had to try and act like the guys that really were after girls, and were doing the girls! Neither one of us ever had any interest in doing the girls. You know, we made up stuff to try and sound like really big shit guys to each other, and around the other guys. Then one day, Jay started telling me about some shit the guys at school were laughing about. It was about these two guys that were 'supposedly' found playing with each other in the locker room. Of course, I really don't know if that ever happened or if that was some story somebody made up. Anyway, we both liked talking about those two guys. We kept making up stuff that they "probably" did to each other. I'm sure we made up more stuff to talk about than what ever happened. After a couple of sessions like that, late at night as we were supposed to be going to sleep, one of us, and yeah – I think it was me – mentioned that talking about guys doing that kind of stuff together was a whole lot more fun than talking about doing something with a girl. Jay said yeah, he agreed. So for months and months then, we actually made up stories about guys doing stuff to each other, just to see who could possibly come up with the wildest stuff. Hey, since neither one of us had ever actually had gay sex, we thought we were really getting real wild on what we made up, but hey, in reality, we were a long, long way from getting into some of the really fun, actual stuff! We just did not have any way to know what really happens in real life."

"We thought, yeah – we 'thought,' that we were just trying to out talk the other person. Actually I know that under each cover, in the dark of the night, we were both supporting good strong hard-ons, but we each knew the other guy couldn't see it, since the room was real dark. This kept up for, probably a year or two. I know damn well both of us were shooting off, either under the covers or in the bathroom, but not letting the other one know about it. At that time we were still trying to act like, 'Oh yeah – big funny talk. Just talk!' Well, I know damn well it was getting both of us excited, but we never talked about maybe us two being gay guys! We just talked about what guys probably do to each other."

"You know how I've told you that Jay hates to wear pants? Well, one day, it was just he and I here at the house, and of course he was naked. I jokingly kept telling him to put some pants on, but I really didn't want him to. I wanted to see his swinger to see if I thought his, or mine, was the bigger. I really never cared if he ran around naked or not! I liked to watch him doing it! To me, the fact that he was a brother – that just never seemed to be of any significant importance. All it was to me – was some guy – running around naked, and his dick was flipping back and forth. All of those made up stories that we had been telling each other, well it started looking like some of them could become reality. I kept telling him to put some pants on. He refused. I really kept up the trying to get him to put them on. Well, anyway, that is what it was supposed to sound like. I know, in my own heart, that what I was actually doing was keeping the subject open, so that I could keep getting more and more vocal about it. I was using that as a gate opener for more than just talk. The more we talked about it, the more I could look at it and not look like I was trying to sneak a peak! Hell yeah, even back then when we were younger, I liked to see his cock and watch it move back and forth. I liked that!"

"While he was running around with his dick hanging out, well actually, nothing to be hanging outside of, but anyway, his dick was out, I would make some comments about some of the stuff that we had talked about at night, over the last couple of years while in bed. I was really trying to see if that talk made him get hard, like it did me. Yeah – it did! Only thing was, that's when he would really try to hide it, or maybe even leave the room if he had to. I know he'd seen mine hard a couple of times, but he didn't want me seeing his – for some reason. Things sure did change later though! Now he wants everyone to see it!"

"Two of our made up guys, that we had made up stories about at night were, "Sammy" and "Sonny." Sammy was always the one with the raging hard-on. So, anyway, one of the times when he left the room, I quietly followed him out to the kitchen. He had gone into the little pantry room. We use it as a storage room now, but anyway that is where he went. I snuck in the kitchen, and then realized that's where he was. I was real quiet and went over to the door and pushed it open, real quick. He had a big boner on! Actually, I had never seen his dick that hard before. I was sure it had been, but he lever let me see it. He had kept it, shall we say, hidden. When I saw it, I laughed and said, "Oh man, shit. You look like our man Sammy. You are raging hard, man! Sonny is not here, what are you going to do with that thing?"

"He was all embarrassed. He had been trying to hide it. Well, then he looked down at my pants and I was showing the same thing, just not out in the open. Then he kind of roughly yelled at me, 'Get yours out man. Yours is stiff too. I'm not the only "Sammy" in here right now. You are hard too, let me see it.' I hesitated. I know I had been wanting to see his hard like this. I was really wanting to reach out and grab it, too, but I guess I felt like I had to act like, 'Oh, no big deal'. No man! It was a big deal to me that day. I had wondered for a long time if his hard dick was kind of like mine, and although I had seen it soft a lot of times, this is the first time that I actually saw it hard. It did look a little longer than mine, but I thought maybe that was because I was looking at it from out in front, and not from down on top of it."

"He yelled again, and this time a little more forcefully, 'Take your pants down, Jake!' I did. I dropped them to the floor, but I had on some undies. They were the loose boxer type, and they truly were standing out as far as the fabric could go. He told me to drop the shorts. He was really getting pretty bossy about this whole thing. I decided that I needed to do as he said, or I was afraid that he might get mad at me. So I dropped my shorts. Shit man – my dick came flying out!

He stood there for a moment and stared at it, kind of like I did with his at first. Then he looked up at me and said something like, 'You like seeing my dick all hard don't you? You've been thinking of me as being Sonny all of these nights, haven't you? I'll bet you've been beating off under your covers when we were talking about Sammy and Sonny, haven't you? I saw a roll of toilet paper in the room one day. That's why that was in there isn't it? So you could clean up your sticky stuff after we talked about what Sammy did to Sonny, right?"

"I had to admit to him that, yeah, that was why it was there, but I actually had thought, up until then, that I had gotten it hidden before anybody else saw it. I rather guess I had not – right?"

"So then Jay looked at me and said, 'Well, brother, I guess we now have two Sammy's in the room, don't we? I guess I'm not the only one that likes to play with my thing. Kind of looks like you like to do the same thing. You like to feel it, right? You think you might like to feel mine to see if they feel the same?' And when he said that, he then grabbed ahold of mine without even acting like maybe he should not do that, nor wonder if I wanted him to do it or not. Oh, shit man! When he put his hand on it, it felt so damn good to me! Right then, if he was a brother or not, did not make any difference to me. I figured we were getting older, hell we were at least 18 or 19 and old enough to decide for ourselves what we wanted to do or not, or have someone else do to us! So some other guy had ahold of my dick, so what!? I had been wanting this to happen for quite some time now. During our talks about our Sammy and Sonny, I guess I had kind of slowly decided that sex with a guy was going to be a lot more fun than sex with a girl. I had really started looking for the day, and for the way that this could happen. Since Jay was the one that was always around me, and was the one that liked to let his dick hang free – as often as he could, I just kind of always figured that if I could just find out for sure that he wanted to play with a guy, instead of a girl, then he would probably be the first one to touch me. And he was!"

"When he grabbed me, I then reached over and grabbed his. I didn't even think about it. I just did it. I guess I had been really anxious to do that, and I now finally had a chance! When I grabbed him, I think that made him get that much harder. Anyway, it felt like it to me. Maybe it was just because it made it kind of jerk when I touched it. He looked at me and asked me how it felt. I told him, it was OK. I didn't want to act too damned excited about it. Then he asked me what I was going to do with it. I kind of looked at him, kind of stupid like I guess, and said, 'I don't know.' I really didn't. I guess I had not thought out that part yet. Once I got ahold of it, then what do I do? Then he shocked the shit out of me! He said, 'Well, I'll show you, what Johnny taught me to do.'"

"God – what a shock I got then! He dropped down in front of me and put my dick in his mouth! That was the very first time that I had ever had any guy touching and playing with my dick, and the very first time I had ever put it in somebody else's mouth! That was the first time for me and gay sex, well hell, sex of any kind except, for jerking myself off!"

"When he went down on it, shit man – my mouth was hanging open so fucking far, that right then, someone could have stuck a dick in my mouth, and I would never have known it. I was shocked shitless! As he started sucking on my cock, I tried to stutter out the question of when did he start doing this? When did Johnny teach him this?"

"I knew who the Johnny was that he was talking about. He was only around for a few hours each week, taking care of a yard for a little old lady down the street. He was then, probably about 22 or 23 years old. Not a real big muscle boy, but had been in sports in high school, so he was still in pretty tight shape. He was a white guy, and he was married! He stood about maybe, five feet, eight inches tall, and weighed probably, maybe like, about, oh – 160 pounds or so. Real cute face on him! Found out later that he had been watching both Jay and I for quite some time. Also – found out that he was not charging Mrs. Adams the full price to do her yard. She had told him that she just could not afford to pay someone to do it for her that year, and since her yard was his only reason to be in the neighborhood, he was doing hers real cheap! He had told her that she simply did not need to be doing that type of hard work herself, so he wanted to help her out. He, of course, never told her why he dropped his price so much. I guess he felt that if he could get to Jay or me, then it was worth it. I guess it worked."

"One day, Johnny drove past our house and found Jay outside. He stopped and made some lame excuse about needing somebody to help him carry some stuff out to the alley that day, and would Jay please help him. Well, once the stuff got carried, that is when he got Jay to go into the garage. And – I guess you could say – that is when he, 'Got to Jay – in the garage'"

"Jay was showing me what Johnny had taught him, but he wasn't sucking on my dick much. He kind of more like – let it slide in and out of his mouth, but shit man it felt good anyway! He did this for probably five minutes or so. I never told him to stop."

"When Jay did finally stop, he told me that Johnny had taken him into Mrs. Adam's garage, and had sucked him off! He said that Johnny, then had Jay put his dick in his mouth, and he taught Jay how to suck and chew on a dick. He said that, 'the Johnny thing' had only happened about a week ago, and Jay admitted that he had not actually sucked any guy off yet. But he was getting anxious to do that. Jay told me that he had decided then, that he was going to find out if I would play with him that way, because when Johnny did it, it was so damn much fun, that he wanted to do it again and he did not want to have to wait for Johnny to be in the neighborhood."

"Shit man," Jimmy exclaimed. "Damn man, what a turn on this is to me. I guess I love hearing about some guy's first time having sex. And to know both of you two, and hear about it, and know what each man looked like, and knowing that you are brothers doing that with each other, that is really hot to me! I really never thought too much about brothers taking care of each other sexually, but man – as I think about you and Jay doing each other, then or now, man that is really turning my buttons on! I wonder if I had a brother, I wonder if he and I could have gotten it on together. Hey, did you and that Johnny guy ever do it together?"

"Oh, yeah man. Often and a lot! Like the next week when Johnny showed up, Jay made sure he was close by, and he told Johnny what had happened between the two of us. God, I guess that got Johnny's crotch all wet. He got Mrs. Adam's yard done very quickly that day! Since he was afraid of doing anything here at this house, he told Jay to come and get me, and to come in the alley way, and to meet him in the garage."

"In between our first time in the pantry room and that day, Jay and I had kind of messed around in our room, once. But that was some pretty lame action, so I have kind of always considered the day in the garage with Johnny as my true second session with a guy. He sucked both of us off that day. He told us, when he had gotten done, that he had never had so much cock in his mouth, in one day. He kept telling us that all the other cocks that he had sucked on were on white guys, ours were the only black cocks that he'd ever sucked on, and he could not believe how much bigger our cocks were than the other ones he's sucked on. And he told us that all of the other guys were older men, and we were a lot younger than any of them. He said, 'Shit man! You add those two cocks together and realize that one guy has had both of them in his mouth in the same day, that is one hell of a lot of cock!'"

"Oh man, this one sounds exciting! I want to hear this, but where is Jay at? Did he run out? I don't want him thinking that we walked away from him."

"No, I'm sure he is probably in the kitchen getting something to snack on, but keep stripping your clothes off, get your ass good and naked, and I will go find him and see what he's up to."

Jake left the bedroom and found Jay with his head stuck in the refrigerator, and of course his bare ass sticking up in the air! Jake slapped his bare ass and told him, "Hey! Jimmy is getting undressed and we're talking about you and I, and our first time together with Johnny. So as soon as I get him all excited telling him about our past playing around, we'll meet you in the basement, OK?"

"In the basement? Are we taking him to the basement today?"

"Yeah, he doesn't know about it yet, but he's a playmate and I don't think there is any reason to try and hide it from him. Hey, man. From what he has already said, he is definitely a heavy player, and we might as well let him know what type of play we enjoy. I'm convinced that it will get him all hot and excited. He is not the type to turn and run. He told me that he hasn't had a chance to play with anybody that has any "equipment," since he moved here. Oh, which reminds me, have you had Patrick in the basement yet?"

"No – no." Jay said, with hesitation. "I haven't shown him that yet! I think the time is getting real close, but even up until now, I have been afraid that if I showed that to him, he might stop his visits. So I decided that I needed to get him a little more in shape with the extra side of gay sex before I showed him the entire 'factory'. So no, not quite yet. Maybe since you know about him, maybe you can help me introduce it to him, without scaring the hell out of him. OK?"

"Yeah, sure! Hell! Sounds like fun to me! We'll do it, but of course you know you are going to have to let him know that I now know about you two. Maybe if we get into some threeways together, that might be a good way to kind of start talking about the basement. We'll get him curious, then take him down there. OK?"

"Shit man, sounds like you have worked this process out before. Have you shown that to someone that I'm not aware of?"

"Hell no man! If so, you would have been down there playing with him too. Hey I'm going back in the bedroom and Jimmy and I will be down in just a few minutes. I'll tell him that you are getting the 'room' ready. I'm sure that will create some questions."

As Jake returned to the bedroom, Jimmy was folding his shorts, and his T-shirt and placing them on a chair.

"Hey Jimmy." Jake said. "Jay had his head stuck in the refrigerator and of course his bare ass sticking up in the air, hoping, I guess that the 'milkman', or somebody, would be looking in the back door window and see the big crack sticking up there. We are going to be using the basement room, instead of the bedroom, so he is getting it ready. I told him we are reminiscing some of my old times."

"OK. The basement room? Should I ask about the basement room? Have not heard about that yet!"

"No, don't worry. It's our, 'fun' room. I think you will enjoy it! We'll introduce you to it shortly. Anyway, the day with Johnny!"

"Jay and I came into the garage through the alley door. I was really nervous. I'd never had anybody but Jay touch my dick before, but I must have been really ready, because I sure didn't take any time getting my clothes off. I had my clothes off before Johnny got done with the yard, and when he came into the garage, there I stood with one damn big stiff hard-on, sticking out in front."

"As Johnny was stripping out of his clothes, he told me, "Get over here boy. Grab that dick of yours, and put it in my mouth!"

"I did as he told me to. He started sucking on it real hard and strong. Nothing like Jay had done a few days earlier. Johnny knew what he was doing, and he was doing good. He motioned for Jay to come over close to us, and when he did, Johnny put his hand up between the spread of Jay's legs and started squeezing Jay's balls. Jay groaned a couple of times, then kind of threw his head back, showing that, that squeezing was feeling good. Johnny had ahold of my nuts too, and he was squeezing them too. Each time he did a good strong suck on my dick, he squeezed my nuts. Damn that felt good. After about 10 minutes of this, he then took his mouth off of my dick, looked up at me and asked, 'So you've never sucked or chewed on a dick yet, right?'"

"I told him, kind of shyly, 'No man, I have not, yet.'"

"Well, now is the time!" Johnny said. "Today you will learn! Jay, get your dick good and hard, your brother is going to be using it for a school lesson here."

"Oh, man! That kind of freaked me out. My brother? Oh shit, I did not expect this. I thought I would be sucking on Johnny's dick, not Jay's. I really wondered if I should say 'No', but for some reason, I just didn't. You know Jimmy, thinking back, I think I really did want to suck on his dick. I think, I kind of knew in the back of my mind that if he and I played together, then we could have sex real often. This was all so new to me, but I knew I wanted to do whatever Johnny said to do."

"Johnny told me to get down on my knees. I did. Then he told me to open my mouth as wide as possible, and to put Jay's dick in my mouth as far as I could. I did. Jimmy, I was real ready for sucking dick! I forgot real quickly who I was sucking on and chewing on. After just a few minutes Johnny asked me if I had been sucking somebody else, before that day."

"I told him, 'No, man. This is the very first time. Why?' Then he said that he had never seen some guy, that has never sucked dick before, go onto a big dick, like Jay's, and work on it so rough and so hard. He told me that I shocked him with how much dick I could take without gagging on it. Then he looked at me and said, 'Jake, you are a natural cock sucker!'"

"I felt kind of embarrassed when he said that, but I managed to look up at him and say, 'Thank you sir!' I have no idea of why I said Sir! I was way too young to understand the 'Sir' thing in a gay relationship. I guess I just respected Johnny so much, that to call him 'Sir', was a natural. Later, when I found out more about the meaning of using 'Sir', I was real glad that I had called him that, that day. I found out later that my using that term, that day, really made him wonder about me and any possible earlier activities."

"Johnny made us stop, before Jay shot off. Johnny told me that he was afraid that if he let that happen during my first sucking session, it might not turn out so well. He was afraid that I could not handle that, and he wanted my first session to be a good one."

"Then he had Jay squat down in front of me and suck on my dick. He kind of gave Jay some instructions on how to go after it a whole lot more aggressively than he had been doing. I was glad. Johnny told him that it was not going to break off. I knew that if Johnny didn't give him some, "Go after it guy" instructions, I sure as the hell was. Jay was being way too mellow and gentle. I wanted it faster and rougher. Jay caught on real quickly. I guess he just needed to be told that going after it like a wild animal was OK. I sure as the hell know it is with me, anyway! That is the way I like it. 'Like an animal!'"

"He stopped Jay short of letting me cum. And, he didn't let me cum when Jay was sucking on me either! We found out why he didn't want either one of us to cum. He was saving it all up for himself."

"While Jay was sucking on me, Johnny started sucking on Jay. Johnny had laid down on the floor, on his back, and had slid up under Jay's butt and got his mouth up on Jay's dick. With the length of Jay's dick, Johnny had to kind of sit up in front of Jay's crotch so that he could get his mouth on Jay's dick. Johnny really went to it. He got Jay real excited! He could tell that Jay was just about to cum, and he quickly pulled off and told Jay to shoot off whenever he was ready, but don't let me shoot. He told me, 'Jake, as soon as I pull off of Jay's dick, after he shoots, you stoop down here and stick your cock in my mouth. Then fuck my mouth. Fuck my mouth real fast and hard. I want your cum in my mouth along with your brother's.'"

"Jay continued to suck on me, but not too wildly since he was told to not let me cum, and Johnny really went to town on Jay's dick. Johnny was taking as much of that dick with every head movement that he could. All of a sudden he felt Jay tense up. He grabbed Jay's butt and pulled himself up and onto Jay's dick, that much closer. Jay shuttered and starting shaking. Then he let out a big moan and a groan and let it fly. I could look down enough to see Johnny really pushing his face up against Jay's crotch. After Jay moaned and kind of shot about three times, then Johnny pulled off of his dick and laid his head down on the floor and kind of mumbled, 'Jake, fuck my mouth! Fast!'"

"With that, Jay pulled off of my dick, and I dropped down so that I could stick my dick down Johnny's throat. I actually just laid across his face and started fucking his face like it was an ass. I fucked him good and hard, and then I felt it all starting. I knew I was getting real close to a cum. I kept pushing and pulling my dick in and out of his mouth. I knew I was just about ready to mix Jay's cum and my own cum together in Johnny's mouth. I remember I kind of said something like, 'Here I come" or some dumb thing like that, and I then really pushed down on Johnny's mouth with my dick, and I really unloaded in him. That was the very first time that I had ever cum in a guy's mouth, well actually anywhere except on my own hand, and I really went for it. Damn, it felt good. I wanted to keep cumming for as long as I could. I really held Johnny down with my crotch laying on his face, and my dick down his throat, as far as possible. Damn, I had found heaven!"

"I did not know it, since I was so wrapped up in what I was doing, but after I pulled my dick out of Jay's mouth, and started fucking Johnny's mouth, Jay continued to stand above us and he beat off, all over again. I had more of his cum all over my back."

"When I got done on Johnny, I was exhausted! All I could do was lay there, and of course – on him. Shit man, he felt so good under me, I was not going to move until I absolutely had to."

"Mrs. Adam's garage was used quite often for the rest of that summer. Hell, Johnny even managed to use the garage for some fake "reason or another," even when he didn't even have to work on the yard. I don't know if Mrs. Adam's ever knew that she was helping Johnny get set up for having sex sessions or not. After the grass cutting season was over, we then had to find times when Mom and Dad were going to be gone and get Johnny over to the house. That's when we started using the basement. Of course, then it was just a big empty room, but we could keep an eye open for the car to drive in the driveway by watching out of the west basement window. If Mom and Dad drove up, then we pulled off of what we were doing and got our clothes on before they got in the house. We always explained Johnny being there as teaching us some wrestling holds. That wrestling mat that we had in the basement, sure came in handy for a lot more use than just wrestling. Of course Jay and I took advantage of every opportunity to suck each other off, as often as possible. So to answer your question, yes – us two brothers do have sex with each other. We do – when there is a third person, and also when there just happens to be a horny guy in the house, that needs to get his rocks off! And for some funny reason, that seems to be quite often! Between the two of us, it seems like one of is always anxious to get his rocks off."

Chapter 4

In the Basement, in the Playroom, and Finally, In-between

As Jimmy and Jake left the bedroom and walked through the house headed for the basement, Jimmy felt rather weird walking through somebody else's house completely nude, but – having his eyes planted on Jake's firm, tight, mahogany, ass muscles, that made him much more comfortable!

Jake turned to Jimmy about half way down the stairs and said to him, "We'll go through the laundry room, and then into the playroom through our rather 'weird' door."

Jimmy saw what was meant about the 'weird' door. As they went through the laundry room, he actually wondered just where they were headed for, since there did not seem to be any way out, except to turn around and go back out, the way they came in.

"We fixed this so that nobody would know the room is here, if we did not want them to know." Jake explained, as he pulled on the edge of a floor to ceiling shelving cabinet and it swung open.

"I guess Jay closed this when he went in so that you could see how secret the room is. Or, maybe I goofed up and he expected me to send you on down here by yourself, and then see how confused you got when you couldn't find the room."

"Wow!" Jimmy exclaimed. "This room really is a secret, isn't it?"

"Yeah," Jake said. "We can tie a guy up and leave him down here for as long as we wish, if we want to."

Although Jimmy knew and could tell that Jake was just kidding, about the tying up part, that is, he replied, "Oh shit man, maybe I had better run now while I can still run! I might find myself being tied up and kept here for a long time." And then added, with a very large grin on his face, "I hope, I hope!"

As he then reached forward and took ahold of one side of Jake's firm, solid, muscular ass, he then continued, "Uh, man, maybe that would not be such a bad thing. Right, Sir?"

As the two entered the room, Jimmy looked around and was amazed at the amount of equipment that was in this small room.

In the center of the room, a room about 12 by 13 or 14 foot, was a sling, along one wall was a counter with all sorts of sex toys laying on the counter and hanging on peg boards above it, and along the far wall was a queen sized double mattress laying on the floor. He could see where there used to be a basement window, but had been very successfully boarded up. The room lighting was, what is available from one 15 watt bulb, and was very soft and low, and as Jimmy adjusted his eyes to the lower light level, he realized that Jay was laying, spread eagle, with his ass in the air, on the double mattress. Jay's mahogany dark skin against the black mattress cover, made him kind of hard to see at first.

"Come on over here guys. Lay down here, Jimmy." Jay rather instructed, as he patted the space on the mattress beside him.

Jimmy and Jake moved over toward the mattress and Jimmy quickly took advantage of the instructions given to him. As he laid down, Jake followed suit and laid down immediately beside him. Jay turned from laying on his stomach to laying on his right arm and gave the two men room, to lie down. Jimmy took a very deep breath. He was now in the position that he had been dreaming about ever since he found out that Jay and Jake happened to be two men, and not just the one man. He was in the middle! He was in a position and a situation now that he had never dreamt possible. Of all of the hot muscular, strong, stud men that he had drooled over in the magazines, he never, ever, imagined himself being in this situation, where it was a reality of some real true living. His thinking of this, and his realizing of its existing reality, was that much more exciting to him when he actually had to kind of stop, somewhat shake his head, and realize that his dream of playing with a very muscular bodybuilder was actually happening. And it was happening with two bodybuilders – at the same time. Two very, very strong, muscular, very well hung, identical twin brothers, that also happened to be two gorgeous black men.

He has always admired the black man body structure, as long as they were an athletic type of a man. He had mentally played with the idea of, finally, finding the right man to be his partner, and the idea of that man being a black man, always made him a little more anxious to find him – than when he just considered the quest in general. He had some prior sexual experiences with men of color, but never in his entire life did he ever happen to think, that within such a very short period of time, actually about maybe less than two hours, would two black men mean so much to him.

Looking over toward Jake, Jimmy said. "Shit man! Ever since I met you, what about five or six weeks ago, I've been dreaming of being in bed with you, but there is no way in hell I can tell either one of you how damn exciting this is to be sandwiched in between the two of you. I thought being with just one of you, when I thought there was just one, was really exciting, but hell, now I am in complete heaven. Both of you please lay up against me. Let me feel your skin against mine. Please, let me feel the two of you all at once!"

Jay was laying with his right hand under the back of his head, and Jake was resting on his left elbow looking over toward Jimmy and Jay. Jimmy reached down and took both of the big, thick, and long black cocks in his hands. He squeezed each. He rather jerked on each. He pulled on each. Then he said, "Shit man, this is way too much to believe! God! Two big thick sticks all at once! Shit man! Which one do I get to suck on first?"

Jay replied, "Go down on Jake's dick. I want to finger your tight asshole while you suck on my brother for a little while, then you can switch over and use my dick."

Jimmy immediately turned himself around so that his ass was now right beside Jay and Jake's faces, and his mouth was right on top of Jake's dick. Still hanging onto Jay's dick, Jimmy grabbed Jake's dick and very slowly started licking around his dick as he admired it up close, as close as a man can get to another man's dick. He then started his descent down the long stiff pole. He placed the tip of Jake's dick in his mouth and slowly ran his tongue around the girth of the dick. The width of his dick made it rather difficult to move his tongue very much or to do too much action on it. As he started to push his mouth down on it, he felt Jay starting the finger action back in his ass. Jay's fingers felt very good and at first very tight in his asshole. That feeling made him that much more anxious to get as much cock in his mouth as quickly as he could. The feeling, of sex, was getting transferred from his ass, through his body, and up to his mouth. He felt the excitement of his entire body having sexual activities all at the same time. The top part of him, and the bottom part of him were both in a state of glory. He felt good all over!

Jimmy lowered his head down onto the cock as he took a very deep breath. He knew that once he had the majority of that enormous dick stuck down in his throat, he would not be able to do any breathing through his mouth. Relaxing his throat, as much as possible, and grabbing onto Jake's mid section and pulling himself forward toward Jake's body, he continued his journey of joy, taking as much dick as he possibly could. Tears rolled down his cheeks as he forced his throat to accept the big stick of meat, that he was now, really, forcing down his throat.

"Shit man!" Jay commented. "Don't you have a hard-on brother? That guy has taken you so damn fast, you must not be giving him a boner."

"Oh man!" Jake replied. "I'm hard as hell. It is a big stiff boner! We just happen to have a playmate here that I guess is used to having his mouth rammed full, and from the way you are playing with his asshole, I guess he is used to having that rammed full too! Is that right, boy?" He directed to Jimmy.

Being unable to speak, Jimmy shook his head in a 'Yes' motion as much as possible and uttered a "Yes Sir" to the best of his ability.

Jake reached down and placed his hands on the back of Jimmy's head. With a slight force, he attempted to help, or maybe force, Jimmy to take even more of his dick. Jay had his right hand on Jimmy's ass, and was slowly poking it with two, then three, and then four fingers. He had repositioned himself so that as his hand worked Jimmy's tight firm ass, he could chew on the left buttock of Jimmy's muscular butt. Each time that he gently bit down, Jake would tell him, "Do that again. That makes our man suck down on my dick harder each time that you do that. Bite him brother! Make him really suck on me real hard. I like that!"

Jimmy was in a position, between the two hot muscular men, to where he was wishing that he could do more stuff, all at the same time. His hands were moving constantly, reaching for some additional part of either human body that he could reach. He really wanted to feel both men, all over, all at the same time.

As he pulled off of Jake's dick, for just a second, Jimmy exclaimed in a very excited manner, "Oh shit men! I never, in my entire life, ever thought that I would ever find myself in such a great situation. Damn I want to do everything all at once. Jay, put as much up in me as you can. Push on my ass!"

"Well – " Jay said. "Dear brother – it sounds to me like our man, wants something a little more than just my fingers up in there. Don't you think?"

"I think you just might be right, big Brother. I think it just might be time to let this tight little ass of his, find out if it's ready for your stick of meat."

Jay grabbed some grease and coated his cock from top to bottom, so that he knew it was in a good slippery condition to go up into Jimmy's tight ass. Jay got himself into position and then told Jimmy, "I'm ready man. I'm about ready to take this ass of yours, are you ready?"

"Oh, hell yes!" Jimmy exclaimed! "Shit yes man. Oh hell yes! This is what I've been waiting on all afternoon! Oh yeah, please fuck my ass! Oh, men! Oh God – how great this is! Please Jay, please, please, put it in me! Fuck me – please!"

And Jay did. He slowly started his decent down into the innards of Jimmy's ass. The head of his dick was bigger than the opening that was so anxious for it, so Jay very gently and lovingly grabbed each side of Jimmy's ass and slightly pulled it apart.

"You doing OK?" Jay asked of Jimmy.

"Oh yeah man. I'm doing good. Yeah man. Hey, Jay. How big is that damn thing, anyway? Do you know?" Jimmy rather queryingly asked.

"Well, the last time that I measured it when it was pretty hard, like it is right now, it was about ten and a half inches long and right at about six inches around. So, it ain't that big man!" Jay replied.

"The hell it ain't that big, man! You two guys are both hung like one overbuilt, fucking bull! That's one hell of a hunk of meat to be ramming up inside of some guy's gut. Jay, I know I can take it. I use dildos on myself larger than that – but that's me – putting 'em in myself. Go slow until you get it all in me. OK? Don't push on it too fast, or too hard at first, OK?" Jimmy rather pleaded to Jay, just visualizing that the rod he was just about to get shoved up in him looked a lot more like a NASA space rocket, standing up straight, getting ready to take off, than like a man's dick! And right then, he was sure that when that thing got shoved up and inside of himself, it was gonna feel like a space rocket blasting off!

"You and your ass are going to be doing just fine." Jay told Jimmy. "This is not going to hurt you any. Your ass is hungry for it! Your ass is looking up at me begging for it, man! Lay down there and just relax your ass. Let it open up for this, and in a minute you and I are going to be, 'one person.' You and me together. You and me, connected together. Me in you, and you taking me in there like I was always supposed to be in there! Me – up in your ass! In just a minute, part of your insides is going to be part of a black man. We are going to make you part white man, and part black man! Now, ain't that exciting to you man? You want a black man up in you, don't you, Jimmy?"

"Oh, hell yes, man! God, Jay! Shit man, I want all of you up in me man, I do! Talking to me that way is really making me kind of crazy. God, that kind of talk is really, really turning me on! Nobody's ever talked that way to me before! Oh, Jay! Damn, that makes me get really, really anxious! Oh shit man, I've got to get you up in me! Oh man! Fuck me! But, it's just that you've got one damn big bull dick that you are gonna be putting up in me, and I want you to go slow for a minute. Your dick back there feels so damn good to me! It's so warm, and it's so stiff and hard, but so damn big! Jay, just keep pushing it, but careful, OK? It feels really, really tight and really, really big back there, but I want it up in me so damn bad! Shit yes I do, damn yes! Just keep pushing on my ass, man. Jake, hang on to me while he gets his damn big pole of a dick, up in me. I'll take it! I know I can take it! But, just be careful in me for a minute, OK?"

Jay laid his body down along the full length of Jimmy's body, and hugged Jimmy, as Jake was also, already doing, from underneath.

Jay reached around Jimmy and got his fingers on Jimmy's tits. As he slowly and gently, started to squeeze them, he told Jimmy, "Here man, maybe this will get your mind off of your ass for a minute, while I put my dick up in there." After he gently started, he then got increasingly more forceful with it, and Jimmy knew that he was getting action, not only in his butt, but on his tits too. Rough, hard, tight, action!

As Jay pinched Jimmy's tits, which made Jimmy squirm and kind of groan, he continued to lower the lower half of his body down onto, and into, Jimmy. Inch by inch, his enormous cock slid up into Jimmy's ass. Jimmy was feeling like nothing better could ever happen, in his entire life. Nothing better than what he was getting to experience right then.

Jimmy was now, the slab of meat, in the middle of the sandwich, that he had been so anxious to become. Under him was one hot, muscular, strong, 'hung like hell', handsome tall black man, and on top of him, and completely imbedded completely into his ass, was the identical twin.

Jimmy realized that one on the top, was another – hot, hunky, muscular, strong, 'hung like a bull', handsome tall black man, that was using his body for his full, total, and complete, pleasure. He knew the one on top was hung like a bull, because he had the entire cock up in himself, and he could feel all of it up in there. Both of these men were hugging him at the same time. His ass was as completely full as possible, his tits were getting pinched very strongly and he was between the two men that he had felt earlier, should be on the cover of muscle magazines. Jimmy felt at that time like there was nothing in the entire world that could possibly go wrong, from that time forward. Jimmy was experiencing the ultimate of sex. This, he knew, could never be duplicated.

Once Jay had penetrated Jimmy's ass to its entire depth, and his cock's entire length, he started in a very slow and methodical fashion of pumping it, for not only his own personal enjoyment, but for Jimmy's complete enjoyment also. Jay started slowly. He listened closely to Jimmy to make sure that his enormous stiff black stick of meat – that he had rammed all the way up and into Jimmy – was still feeling comfortable to Jimmy, after being rammed that far up into his ass. When he decided that everything was OK, he then started a much more aggressive fucking campaign in Jimmy's ass. He started pumping full force.

"Hey Jake, my man." Jay told Jake. "I've got all of my dick up in this tight little ass now, and I've kind of rammed him a couple of times, and I think he is now ready for some good fast and fun action! Listen to him carefully, just in case I get too rough. Let me know if he says anything that I need to know. I'm about ready to – 'take this fucking to the city,' man! Here I go!"

With that statement, Jay started to use Jimmy's ass to his complete and unbelievable, enjoyment and pleasure. Jay was a strongly built man, and he was definitely using his strength in doing this fucking. Jimmy was getting the fucking of his life – by a very, very strong man. A man that can take control and use it to his advantage!

Jake grabbed ahold of Jimmy and told him, "Jimmy, you are about to get your ass taken care of like it probably has never been taken care of before! That man that has got his cock up in your ass, loves to fuck and he loves to fuck real hard! He is really going to be slamming your ass, hard! If he gets too rough, let me know, OK, man?"

"Oh shit, man!" Was about all Jimmy could say. "Oh shit, man! Oh, God man, that feels so damn good up in me. Oh, shit Jay! Ram my ass man! Oh man, I want to know you are up in there and using me! Fuck me man! Fuck me hard! Oh God man! Oh yes, thanks Jay. God, you feel so damn good doing that! Hey – Jake. After he does me, will you do me then? Will you get on me? Do me like Jay is fucking me, OK?"

"Hell yes, I will, man – if you think your ass will be able to take more fucking after my brother is done back there. The way he is slamming your asshole right now, I really wonder if your butt is going to want my dick or anybody else's dick up in there for awhile."

"Jake, my ass might be sore after he gets done, but I want to know that I got fucked by both of you guys the first time that we got together. I want to know that I got it from both of you. I'm kind of like that Johnny was the time he sucked both of you guys off. He wanted to mix your cum and Jay's cum together in his mouth. I want to mix it together up in my ass. Jake, my ass might really hurt by the time we are done, but that will be OK with me. I will know that I got it the way I wanted it! OK, man?"

"Yeah sure! If you don't mind walking around with an aching asshole, hell yes, I'll get in there and unload too. You know Jay – for Jimmy looking like such a 'prim and proper' type of a guy, he sure is the hottest ass, and the most damned anxious ass I think we have ever played with. Shit man – I don't ever remember any other guy that begged for both of our dicks during the same session. Hell man, every one of them that I can remember playing with, refused the idea of getting fucked by both of us. They'd take one of us and then say no more. This guy is just plain damn hungry back there!"

"Yeah, brother, he is! And right about now he is about to get some of that hunger taken care of! Hold him tight brother – give him some loving, man! I'm about ready to do it to him, man! I'm about ready to let his ass have it! It's cummmin – it's cummmming man! Oh shit, man! Oh man, oh he just got a load and a half! Oh man – if he still wants your dick, get ready because I have done my dumping back here. Let me lay here for just a minute to recoup and then you can fuck the hell out of him! Man, all I can say is – if he wants both of us up in there, then we've got to help the poor guy out. I'll tell you though, I don't know how in the hell his ass can take that much abuse again, though! I'm sure my ass couldn't! Jake, you ready to change places, man? Jake, get ready for some hot ass fucking, man! His ass is begging like you ain't never, had an ass beg before!"

"Jimmy," Jay said. "You are about to get another big fucking bull cock rammed up in your ass, man! He's hung just like me, so get ready for another big bull cock up in your butt!"

Jay and Jake switched places, and much more quickly than Jay did, Jake rammed his meat pole up into Jimmy's ass end. He had decided that this guy was real hungry for the big, strong, thick, stiff, black, meat rod, and he was willing to provide another one. Having been the guy on the bottom, holding and playing with Jimmy, as Jimmy got his first rough fucking, Jay had gotten very hot and anxious for his chance at Jimmy's ass. He had a ragging hard-on! Stiffer than he could remember it being, for quite sometime.

Jake started in on Jimmy as if his cock was the first cock up in that ass, that day, and he did not bother to ask if everything was OK. He knew brother Jay was holding Jimmy tightly and if anything was going wrong, Jay would know. Jake was bouncing both of the guys on the bottom with his forceful fucking. He was pounding hard. He was getting all of the rough fucking out of his system that he could, and as quickly as he could. He had a man under him that was asking for it, and a man that was anxious to get whatever he could get, so Jake was willing to deliver.

"Shit man!" Jay said. "God, man! Jake, if you fuck him any harder, he and I both are going to have trouble getting up from here. Shit man, God, – can his ass take anymore of this? Shit man, his ass has got to be really hurting! Hell, I thought I fucked him hard. Shit man – damn! You are going to give yourself a heart attack if you don't slow it down a little."

"No, No!" Jimmy kind of shouted. "No, don't let him slow down any! Please keep it up! Oh man! Pound me man! My ass has never been treated this well and I really want it. Please Jake, keep fucking me good and hard, man! I really want this! Oh men, oh shit! I can't believe this! Oh man! Earlier today I had no idea that I would get anything like this, ever in my whole life! And oh – man – today – I'm getting it! Oh men. I'm so damn glad I went to the gym today! Oh, please promise me that we can do this a lot! Please! Please!'"

"Yeah – we will man!" Jay reassured Jimmy. "We will! Brother and I have now found ourselves a real active and anxious asshole to play with, that feels real good to us too, and yes man, we are going to be using you a lot. You might think you are getting it for your pleasure, but you need to know that I think both of us are feeling like you have got one of the nicest, tightest little assholes around here, and we are going to make you be, the little white asshole, in the middle of the two black brothers, just as often as possible!"

"Hang on to him, man! Squeeze him Jay! I'm going to unload here in just a minute. He wanted to be the Mixmaster of our cum shots, and he is about ready to get the second load! God man – Jay. You telling him how we are going to be using him, and having him play with us a whole lot, really got me all turned on! Just the idea of hearing you say that – got me all excited. Hang on to him man! It's coming! It's coming! I'm cumin man! I'm cumin! Oh shit, man! Oh shit man, I just loaded you man, I did! Oh Jimmy, can you feel the juices I just loaded you up with?"

"Oh shit, yes I can! Oh hell yes, I can! And it feels so damn good in me! Oh Jake, push on my ass as hard as you can man. Oh yeah – drill that damn big pole up into me. Oh shit man, push, push, push! Oh yeah! Oh men! Oh shit! Oh God that feels so damn good up in me! Oh, I wish I could just keep your cock up in my ass all of the time. Oh men! Oh, guys – thank you both, for doing me! Oh, man, how in the hell can any one guy ever dream of getting himself in this kind of a place where he is fucked by two of the hottest built guys in town, or in the country. Two brothers, that are just plain hot, hot, hot muscle guys, that just happen to be beautiful mahogany identical twins, and they both just happen to have sticks of death hanging on them! How can a guy ever dream of more?"

"Well – let me tell you something – little white guy. You ain't so bad yourself, man. Yeah, you look a little pale compared to brother and I, but a 'pine-white' ass is just as good to fuck as a black ass is. It ain't the color of the ass, it's the action of the ass! And let me tell you something young man, you have got one hell of an active, hungry and deep ass! Shit man, you really like to have that ass played with, and played with good and strong! Jake and I have never had a guy in bed that can take it and beg for it like you do. You want it, and you know you want it. And you ain't afraid to let us know that you want it. I hope you realize that we are both very willing to give it to you! Brother Jake and I have been looking for some guy like you for a long time now. We have been trying to find some guy that can really take it and really like it. Somebody that can take one of us, and then beg for the other guy, too. Yeah, we play with each other, and we get pretty active doing each other, but that's because we haven't had the right third guy here with us. We've been trying to find that third guy that likes it good and rough too. I kind of think that maybe you showed us today, that you are 'the' guy that we have been looking for. Jake and I did not know if it was going to be a white guy or a black guy, and I kind of think it might have turned out, to be a white guy. Jake, I think maybe we just completed the ole Oreo cookie thing! Don't you?"

"Oh yeah, brother. I do! A little white icing in between two black cookies, makes for a pretty good combination. Don't you think, hey Jimmy? You don't mind being a little white icing do you?"

"Oh man! I will be the white icing, anytime that I can! Hell yes! Hey guys, earlier today when I kind of found out that maybe – just maybe I was going to get to come home with you guys, that is what I thought about. The three of us making a human Oreo cookie. I wanted to be the middle of an Oreo cookie!! And – course – you know that meant that I had to be the middle guy! Oh men, I will be the icing whenever I can! Somebody can push me up between the two of you and just get me all trapped in the middle, anytime! I will never complain about that squeeze! And you know too, how people love to lick the icing in an Oreo cookie!"

"OK men." Jake rather managed to lowly say. "This part of that cookie is kind of whipped after the way I took care of the icing in the middle. My dear brother – is damn right! You are one hot active guy, and I know for damn sure, your ass is going to have calluses inside of it from all of the action that our dicks are going to be giving it! If you like getting fucked by these two dicks of our, then we've got a real thing going here. We've been trying to find us a guy that wants to get fucked by both of us, and you are the first one that will take one of us and then beg for the next one! You are one hot hungry toy! I hope you don't mind being referred to as a toy – but that is what you became today! You are better than going to some toy store and spending money on some fancy type of a play toy! Jimmy, you are a real live talking and kicking toy, one that can he fucked over and over again, and then come back for more later! No toy maker can make something as good as you and this ass of yours!"

"Men – you can call me a pile of junk if that's what it takes to make me your number one toy boy. Men, my ass has never – ever – felt this good, and it is now ready and willing for either one of you, or both of you, whenever either one of you need it or want it."

Jay had, by this time, gotten himself up off of Jimmy and the three men were now back laying beside each other on the mattress.

"Shit men, my ass feels good, but it really feels empty now that both you guys have had your enormous bull cocks up in it." Jimmy told his two hunky, hung, playmates.

"Well, it don't have to stay empty unless you want it to, Jimmy." Jay said.

"Uh – what do you mean?" Jimmy asked.

"Well, just because Jake and I have worn our cocks to a frizzy, up and inside of your ass, if your ass is still hungry, we've got plenty of stuff around here that we can put up in there if you like. Hey, it doesn't have to stay empty. We can stuff it with any kind of stuff, to keep it feeling nice and full!" Jay replied.

"Like what?" Jimmy rather laughingly asked. "Yeah, my ass is still available and could still be played with if anybody is interested. You guys will find out, I love to get played with, and today sure is my kind of a day. If you guys want to play with it some more, I'm willing!"

"Yeah. From what he is saying, I think maybe a butt plug might be a good thing to use on him, right now. Don't you?" Jay asked Jake.

"I don't hear him trying to tell us no, so I would assume that he agrees about that. Is that right, young man?"

"I'm game men. I love you guys playing with me, and I'm your toy, as you guys just said. A toy to be played with!"

Jay said to his brother, "Hey, Jake, reach over there and grab that medium sized butt plug out of that storage basket, and some grease too."

"Jay, are you sure he can take that much up there? Especially after the fuckings that he just got. That one is kind of wide!"

"Yeah, he'll take it, I'm sure. His ass might not be open far enough for it right now, but after I play with it some more, I'm sure it will be very anxious to take probably this one and maybe either the large plug or one of the dildos."

"Right man?" He once again directed toward Jimmy.

"Well, yeah I guess, but since I'm not sure of just what size you are talking here, I'd better be careful of what I say."

"Hey this butt plug is only about 8" around. It's of course not too long. I think it will fit up in your ass real nicely!"

Jimmy had asked if whichever one was not going to be putting the plug in his ass, if he could suck on his dick while the other brother plugged his ass with the plug. Jake agreed, and quickly went out to the little bathroom that was there in the basement and kind of washed his dick off, and then returned to the sex scene, and proceeded to get his cock in just the right place for Jimmy to do a complete suck job on it.

Jake looked over at Jay as he handed him the plug and the grease and said, "Well man, about all I can say is this young man is really up to getting his ass spread and opened – so fill his ass up brother! Just take it nice and slow. Remember, I've got my dick stuck in his mouth, and if you ram him too fast or too hard, he just might bite me. So let's take care of my dick, OK?"

"Oh yeah, brother! I like the way you think. Force the poor guy's ass open as far as possible, and don't worry about if he can take it or if it hurts or not, but don't let him bite your poor little dick! Just for that, I might just slam and ram his ass with this plug as fast and as hard as I can, just so he will bite on your dick as hard as he can. Maybe that's what I should do!"

With that statement, Jay and Jake looked at each other, then looked toward Jimmy, then back to each other again and both just kind of shrugged their shoulders as if to say to each other, "Hey man. He's not bitching any. He's not complaining. I guess he's really ready for whatever happens back here."

Jake then told Jay, "Well, go for it man. I think we have an asshole here that is willing to take anything that we can give it!"

Hearing that statement, Jimmy attempted to utter an agreement. He was in a sex play session that he was going to enjoy to the utmost, and he was not going to tell either man to, not do something, whatever, that man wanted to do. He was completely surrendering his body to these two muscular hunks, and he was ready for anything.

Jay greased up the butt plug and started it in between the cheeks of Jimmy's ass. Jimmy took as deep of a breath as he could, through his nose, in anticipation of getting his ass opened up, and not being too sure of how quickly it would be happening, nor being sure of just how big and thick, an eight inch around plug feels like. He did not know exactly how far open his ass was going to be spread, but he knew he was gonna feel it, and feel it big!

Being in bed with these two men, being played with by both of them, being their center of attention, having both of them touching him and rubbing him, fucking him, and having as much dick stuck down his throat as he had, simply made him loose all self control. His anxiety, of being their toy, was making him submit his entire existence to them – for them to use and play with – to their complete enjoyment. He was offering his body as a toy! He was actually thinking, 'I'm just a toy, men! Play with me and use my body! Forget I'm a man. I'm only a play thing that can feel good to you. Use me! Use me! Have fun with me! Pull me, spread me! Today, I am yours! I am just a toy!'

As the butt plug started its travel up into Jimmy's ass, Jimmy jerked as the tip entered his asshole. He slightly bit Jake's dick. He attempted a muttered, "I'm sorry."

Jake realized what was happening, and he actually was enjoying it, getting bitten or not. He told Jimmy, "No problem man. If he forces your ass too far too fast, you can bite me as hard as you want. I'll know that way how my brother is treating your ass. And, besides, I think Jay is trying to make me learn to like having my dick bitten, as hard as he or some other guy can bite it, so I'm sure he is going to make sure I have my fill of getting 'cock bitten', before we are done."

Jay pushed the plug in a little, then stopped. He heard Jimmy groan. Then he pushed it in a little farther. Jimmy jerked, let out a little groan, and again bit Jake. Jay knew Jake had gotten bitten when he jerked and let out somewhat of a small groan.

"Did you get bitten, brother? Did your dick just get bitten?"

"Yeah, a little, but no problem. I didn't expect it, but once he did it, it actually felt good. I don't know, maybe I do like getting my cock bitten, don't I, man?"

"OK brother. Get ready to really get bitten then, because I'm going to slam the rest of this up in his ass, and I know he is going to feel it when the wide part slams in."

Once again, directed to Jimmy, Jay asked. "You ready man? It's not that much fatter than the cock that you've had up in there today, so you will take this real easily!"

Jimmy attempted another head shake of a 'Yes, I'm ready."

Without any further comments, Jay turned to look at Jake and rather gave him a nod of, "OK man, here goes!"

Jake shook his head as if to say, "OK man, do it."

Jay leaned down and bit Jimmy's left buttock, and as he still had Jimmy's skin in his teeth, he suddenly, forcefully, pushed the plug. It went in! It snapped in! Jay continued to push on the end so that Jimmy could feel the pressure of it in his ass, and also so that Jimmy could not attempt to push it back out. He heard Jimmy rather cry in a muffled tone. He knew that had hurt Jimmy's ass. He knew this 8" around plug definitely felt a whole lot bigger than the 6" around cocks that had been pushed up in there just a little while ago. He knew Jimmy's ass felt like it had just been torn open. He also knew Jimmy had asked for it. He knew he was doing what Jimmy was wanting. He knew he was getting a little more than just 'kind' of rough with Jimmy, but he knew he was not going beyond what Jimmy was asking for, and was ready for. This was turning Jay on. This was really turning Jay on! He was liking what was happening. He decided that he had never been quite this rough with any other guy before. He realized that getting this rough with another guy's ass, and another guy's body, was really a hot turn on to him.

Jimmy, jumped and jerked. He straightened out his body. He bit Jake very strongly. He attempted to yell, and at the same time threw his head down onto Jake's dick even stronger. He groaned about three loud groans. He grabbed Jake's body and hugged it. He attempted to breath as deeply as possible, and then completely laid his face down on Jake's body and kind of whimpered in pain. His ass hurt!

Jay knew Jimmy was in pain. He also knew that the pain would be only for a few seconds, but while it was there, he knew it hurt. And he knew it hurt badly. He immediately threw himself across Jimmy's body and hugged him so that Jimmy would know that Jay cared.

"Is your ass OK?" Jay asked.

As much as possible, Jimmy attempted to tell him, "Yes" but of course still had that big piece of meat stuck down his throat, and really could not talk.

Jay turned to Jake and asked. "Well, brother, how is your dick? I have a very strong feeling that you have just been bitten."

"Yeah, I got bitten, big time, but I don't think I felt as much pain as Jimmy did. He's one tough little player isn't he Jay? He can really take it. I think maybe we ended up with a gold mine, finding him. And, the way you were playing with him, and his ass, I now kind of think that maybe my brother could get into the real rough stuff, couldn't he? Is that something that you have been hiding from me?"

"Yeah, I guess so. Getting that rough back there was a real hot turn on to me. I've never rammed any other guy's ass that hard, before. I liked that! Yeah, I will agree with you that he is a gold mine, and a gold ass! I don't remember having anybody else down here that plays like this one does. Shit man! He hasn't even taken that dick of yours out of his mouth yet, either. Usually guys will complain that they need to come up for air long before this. After we get your cock out of his mouth, and he can talk again, we need to find out just how rough he likes to play. I sure do hope that today is not some kind of a fluke with him. The way he is taking stuff up his ass today, he might be a candidate for that damn big Elmer-dildo, that nobody else has been able to take up in their ass yet."

"Oh shit!" Jake replied. "Do you think he will be able to take that damn big thing?"

"Well, I don't know for sure, but I sure in the hell, do want to find out!" Jay replied. "Right now – his ass is acting like it is the closest one, more than any other ass we've ever tried – into maybe actually being able to take it. And, I think that ass can open up far enough to take it! I know damn well his ass is hungry for it! Isn't it, Jimmy?"

Chapter 5

Well, it's up to you man!

Jimmy could hear everything that was being said, and he liked it. He liked the fact that he was being talked about and his actions were being rather graded by these two unbelievable, brother, hunks. He decided that maybe he had finally found himself, at least, one playmate that could get it going in a real rough and ready and roaring manner! He was now getting anxious to find out if Jake could get as rough as Jay does. Until now, about all Jake had done during this butt plug session, was lay there with his enormous dick sticking up in the air, but he did admit that he liked getting it bitten. And he was kind of referring to liking it bitten, really firm and really hard!

Jimmy was not so sure of just how big of a dildo they were talking about, but he was getting really excited with just the talk that was going on about if he was going to be able to take it up in his ass or not. He had never had himself in such a situation like this before, where two guys were judging his abilities, and guessing if he could actually take a particular item up in his ass or not!

Jimmy pulled off of Jake's cock and asked, "Hey guys, what size of a dildo are we talking about here?"

"About nine and a half inches around at the head, and about 12 or 13 inches long. That's all!" Jay replied.

"Oh shit!" Jimmy answered. "Damn man! That's big around the head. Shit man, if you guys want to see if I can or not, I'm your toy today, but damn I'm afraid my ass is going to be really split open. I know the 12 or 13 inches of length is not going to be a problem, I take skinny dildos that long, but shit man, that's going to be a damn thick shaft, and that 9 and a half inches around is big! That, I know, is really going to be stretching my ass, way open."

"Well, it's up to you man! Jake and I will try it on you, or should I say, in you, if you want, but you have to tell us if you want to or not."

"I guess you guys do have one like that right? I mean, I guess if you want to try it in me, then you must have one right?"

"Oh yeah, man. We have one!" Said Jay. "We've got one, but nobody has ever had it up in his ass yet. We've tried it on a couple of guys, but their asses just would not open up far enough. You want to be our next attempt?"

"Yeah, I do. Yeah, let's try it. I'm probably out of my mind for saying yes, but damn it, it sounds like fun. And playing with you two guys all at the same time has got me so damn hot, I'll probably agree to do stuff that at any other time, I would not do. Now when we do this, if I decide that I just can't take it, will you stop? I mean, I really want to try, but just in case!"

Jimmy was truly somewhat afraid of his capabilities of taking that much dildo up his ass, and also the associated pain that would come with it. But, his excitement of having these two muscular, statues of men, playing with him, just made him want to be admired by both of them. Jimmy was so afraid that he could turn out to be just another normal playmate to these two identical muscular hunks, that he was admitting to himself, that he was willing to go way beyond normal bounds, just to become something special to these two men. Jimmy truly wanted to become something special to these two men, and he was willing to go the 'extra length', to do that.

"Yeah, we'll stop if you say to." Jay answered. "Hey, Jake, get the dildo while I take this butt plug out of Jimmy's ass and kind of rub his ass nice and lovingly, so that he, and his ass, knows we really do love him and that ass!"

Jake got up and crossed the room to get the dildo, and a can of grease to be used on, and in, Jimmy's ass, and of course to completely cover the dildo with.

"I'm going to pull this plug out, man." Jay told Jimmy. Are you ready? It'll snap when it comes out. Get ready to grit your teeth!"

"Oh shit! Damn! Oh God! Oh shit! Damn!" Jimmy screamed as Jay pulled the butt plug out of his ass.

"Are you OK? I told you that I knew it was going to hurt. Here lay still for a minute. Let me give it some loving. Let me rub it."

"Oh shit." Jimmy exclaimed. I knew it was going to hurt some when it came back out, but damn man, I guess I just was not expecting it quite that fast. I guess I didn't know you were going to pull it out quite then, or that fast. I'm OK now. Well, kind of. My ass still hurts, but not like it did there for a second. Let me lay here for a minute before we do anything else with my ass, OK?"

"Yeah, man. Lay there and relax. I guess maybe I should have told you that I was going to pull it out when I did. Here let me rub your butt. I'm sorry, man. I did not mean to hurt you like that!"

"Hey, that's OK Jay. It just hurt for a second or so, but damn it was a sharp pain. Hey, man. I'm into this man play because it's the rough and tumble way to have sex, so I need to remember that once in awhile, it gets wild. I'm here because I want it, so I need to just accept

– that part of it might be a little painful once in awhile. I don't like mellow, calm, vanilla sex, so I get what I ask for. Right man?"

"Yeah, you are right! Wild sex play can get on the rough side. I guess maybe all of us like it that way, or we would not be playing together, right?"

"Right! I'm sorry I was such a cry baby. Jake have you got that big dildo about all greased up so that you and Jay can make me be a good, big, boy now?"

Jake turned from the counter cabinet area and was finishing up putting grease on the dildo. As he turned, Jimmy got his first glimpse of it.

"Oh shit! Oh God! That damn thing is big, isn't it?" Jimmy exclaimed. "Damn man! God, can my ass open up that far? Which one of you guys is going to try and push that damn thing up in me?"

"Well, I don't know." Jay said. "Why, does it make a difference?"

"No, it doesn't make any difference to me, but I want one of you laying under me so that I can grab onto one of you while I'm trying to take that thing. Can we do that? Can I lay on top of one of you, like when I was getting fucked?"

"Yeah, you can, man." Jake replied. "Jay, you do his ass, and I'll lay down so he can lay on top of me. I'll hang onto him, and try to keep him in place. Is that what you want, Jimmy?"

"Yeah, whichever, of you muscle hunks, I don't care. I just know I am going to need some help trying to keep me in place so that I don't keep scooting away when you guys try to ram that up in me."

Jake laid down, and positioned Jimmy on top of himself. Jake but his arms around Jimmy, and gently squeezed him. "Is this what you want Jimmy?"

"Yeah, thanks Jake. I know I am going to need you hanging on to me, if I can take that thing. I hope I can do this. I've never been fisted before, and from the looks of that damn thing, I have a feeling that if I can get that up in me, then I'll have had something bigger than a fist up in my ass. Right?"

"Oh!" Jake said. "I had been wondering if you had ever had a hand up in there, so I guess that kind of answers that questions, don't it? Ready Jay? We've got us kind of a virgin ass back there. Let's get him ready for other things that will be happening down here in the future. We sure don't want some virgin ass running around here when we have the fisting parties. Now do we?"

"Oh shit! Do you guys have fisting parties?" Jimmy rather excitedly, inquired!

"Well, only when we can find some good empty asses that want to be filled up. So maybe after today, we will have another one." Jay said. "Are you guys ready? I'm starting to get anxious to see if we can get this up in this ass or not."

"Ready here." Jake said.

"Yeah, ready – I think!" Jimmy kind of softly said. "God, Jake! Grab me tight! Oh shit man, I hope I can do this!"

As Jimmy grabbed Jake, and Jake started to squeeze Jimmy, Jay started to spread Jimmy's ass cheeks, and rubbed some additional grease up into his asshole.

"I'm putting a lot of grease up in your back-end tube, man." Jay said.

After Jay loaded Jimmy's ass with a load of grease, he then positioned the tip of the dildo up against Jimmy's asshole. He started pushing, and turning the dildo at the same time. He pushed the dildo as firmly as he could, and attempted to open Jimmy's ass as widely as he possibly could.

"Hold him tight, brother." Jay said. "I'm going to be pushing pretty hard down here, trying to get that cute little asshole to open up. Are you guys ready? Jimmy, are you ready to have a great big hole back here, man?"

"Oh shit, man!" Jimmy again said! "Damn man, I hope I can get it in."

With Jake holding Jimmy very firmly, and Jay playing as, the great clap of thunder from above, Jimmy very slowly began to take the dildo, a little at a time. Jay re-greased the dildo twice, and re-started his entry after each greasing. Jimmy knew that progress was being made, he knew his asshole was opening up farther and farther, each time that Jay pushed on the dildo. He could tell that he had a bigger, open, asshole back there than he had ever felt before. He knew that Jay was putting his hand up in Jimmy's ass each time he took the dildo out to re-grease it, and each time he could feel more hand going up in him, farther, and farther, before Jay put the dildo back up in him. He knew his ass was coming open in a big, big way.

"Jake, hold your man firm. I'm about ready to snap the head of this thing in his ass. He is going to feel it."

"I've got him." Jake replied. "Go for it. Our man is ready. He's been whispering in my ear that he wants it! He's anxious! Do it man!"

With that last "Do it man," Jay pushed really hard, and the head of the dildo went into Jimmy's ass. Jimmy jumped! Jimmy grabbed Jake and squeezed him very hard. Jimmy let out a small scream. Jimmy kept screaming in a low tone, "Oh shit man! Oh shit man! Oh shit man! Oh shit man!"

"It's up in him." Jay said. He's got the head of it up in his ass! Squeeze him tight! I'm sure his ass is really hurting right now!"

"Oh God, yes it is!" Jimmy kind of cried. "Damn man! Oh shit man! God, maybe I should have just had a hand put up in there.

It could not feel any worse! Oh my sore ass! Oh man, Jay, Jake, will my ass quit hurting pretty soon?"

"Yeah, just lay there for a minute man." Jake told him. "Jay's just letting the dildo lay there in your ass without moving it for a minute or so, and you will be OK in a minute. Just hug me. Oh, yeah, man! Also think about how much you have up in your ass right now, and that will take your mind off of the pain. You've got a bigger ass full right now than you have ever had before. Especially, if you have never been fisted."

"Oh man." Jimmy replied. "The next time I feel this much up in my ass, I am going to make damn sure it is going to be one of your fists. Shit, right now, I wish that is what was up in there. Hey guys, tell me something."

"Yeah?" Jake asked.

"Since I've gotten this thing up in me, can I be invited to one of your fisting parties, now?"

"Hell yes, man!" Jay and Jake both responded. Jay continued, "Shit man, you're the only guy that we have ever been able to force this up into. You will be our trophy boy when we have a party. I'm going to hang a sign on your back that points to your ass and says that it has taken the big dildo! Every fister here will want to play with your ass."

Having some light hearted conversation gave Jimmy's ass some time to relax and accept the big toy that was still up in there.

"You OK now, man?" Jay asked.

"Yeah, my ass sure feels full! Kind of like I really need to go take a shit – but it quit hurting!"

"OK, I'm going to move it around some, so that you can feel it up in there, and then also see if we can put anymore of it up in you, and farther. OK?"

"Yeah! Yeah, I want to see if you can get it up in me any farther now that it's past my asshole. I'd like to see how far up in me you can get it, if possible."

Jay continued to play with the dildo, and did manage to get about three or four more inches, up and into Jimmy's ass. Each time it moved in a little farther, Jimmy would grab Jake and squeeze him. But, each time he did that, he laid his head down on Jake's shoulder and told Jake how excited he was that he was getting more of it up in himself. He kept telling him that he wanted to show both of them how much he could take. He was feeling proud of himself for being able to take this dildo, especially since they had said that nobody else had been able to get it in their asses.

Jimmy told them, "Guys, I want to be your 'Special Boy'! I want to be your number one playmate and toy!"

After about 15 minutes of playing with the dildo up in his ass, Jimmy did have to admit that his ass was getting really kind of sore.

"Yeah, I thought it should be." Jay said. "Now Jimmy – when I pull this back out – it's gonna hurt again. When it comes back out, it's got to open up your asshole again, to get the head of it back out of you. But since you'll be able to squeeze your ass shut right away, it won't hurt as much or as long as it did when I put it in. OK?"

"OK. Grab me Jake. Grab me tight!" Jimmy said. "Pull."

Jay pulled the dildo out, and Jimmy jerked and grabbed ahold of Jake and squeezed him. He did not let out as many moans and groans as he did when Jay pushed the dildo up in him. He did squeeze Jake very tightly!

Jimmy relaxed across Jake's body, and Jay turned to lay the dildo on the counter. As he did, he told Jake, "Well, brother, I guess we will not have to find out now, how rough he plays, will we? He's the only one we've ever had down here that was man enough to get that damn big thing rammed up in his ass, so I guess we should assume that he's game for about any damned thing we want to do. Agree?"

"Agreed, brother, agreed! What about you Jimmy? Do you agree that you are up for about anything that might be happening?"

"Shit, what else could happen to me? I think I just took the damn kitchen sink up in my ass, so hell, whatever, whenever, I guess I'm game!"

"Jimmy, have you had enough action for one afternoon?" Jake asked. "That is if we promise that today is not the first and the last of our sessions together?"

"Hey man, that last part was the important part. The doing this again, I mean. I feel like I was the complete taker, this afternoon though! Shit, I got fucked by both of you guys – then you played with my ass and that butt plug – then you rammed that damn freight train of a dildo up in there! I'm the one that got all of the good stuff today! The two of you took care of me so damn good, but I feel like it was just all me. I feel like I need to pay back, someway!"

"Oh man!" Jay replied. "Do not worry about that any. We have found ourselves a real playmate that really knows how to play, and we will be taking great advantage of that. I've been having fun with Patrick for the last year, but shit man, I've really been anxious to really get it on, and he is just not the right guy. You are! You are wild, and I like that! You and I are going to have some damn hot sessions, and I'm sure Jake will not be left out of the picture. Right Jake?"

"You are damn right, brother. I know you are going to be taking advantage of Jimmy while I am out of town, but when I am here, he is mine to play with. When I am here, you, dear brother, will have to ask my permission to play with him. Understand?"

"Uh – yeah. I guess I do. I didn't know this was turning into an ownership arrangement, but hey, life is life."

Both brothers turned and looked at Jimmy. They were each very interested in seeing what Jimmy's reaction was, to those comments. Jimmy had a smile on his face!

"Uh – this shit doesn't bother you any?" Jake asked Jimmy. "I mean, we are kind of talking about ownership here – ownership of you! You're not freaking out about the way we are talking about you? We're really trying to find your limits here, and man, you are starting to freak me out with the way you are willing to do anything we say."

"Shit no!" Jimmy responded. "Hell man! Earlier today I did not even have any remote idea of the possibility of getting in bed with either one of you. Although I only knew about one of you then. And now I have the two hottest, sexiest, muscular, hung studs, that just happens to be brothers, kind of attempting to claim ownership of me! Shit man! I'm not upset! This is making me so damn horny all over again, I'm about ready to let one of you fist me, just to show my excitement. Fight over who gets to play with me. I love it! I've never had this happen before! Damn man! That turns me on! Do you guys, either one of you realize how many millions of men are out there right now, wishing that they were the guy that was getting talked about like this, by you two guys?"

Laughing, Jay said. "Well, dear brother, I don't think this one is going to get very upset if one of us tries to claim ownership over him. Shit man, I think he is so damn anxious to play with either one of us again, he doesn't care what the rules are."

Then he turned to Jimmy and said. "Put, there is one rule that I will personally lay down for you when you are over here with me!"

"Yeah – what is that?" Jimmy asked.

"When you are over here with me, there will be no clothes wearing, going on. Understand? I run around with my bare ass hanging out, and my dick flipping back and forth, and you will do the same thing! Agreed? Understand?"

"Sir, no problem there! I like to be naked as much as you do, so no problem there! My bare ass is not as hot as yours, and my dick don't flip and flop around as much as yours, but I'll run naked too. Fact is, if I can do that over here kind of freely, I might be here most of the time. I can't get away with that at my place, and I really do like to be naked as much as possible."

"Deal man! Anytime you feel like you've had clothes on too much, you just get your butt ass over here, and we will run around naked together."

"Hey Jimmy." Jake broke in. "Why don't we take you out in the laundry room and wash some of that grease off of you. Jay, you start getting things cleaned up in here while I go wash his ass, and then we will meet you upstairs and find something for supper. That OK with you Jimmy?"

"Shit yes!' Jimmy answered. "Especially that part about you washing the grease out of my ass! I thought I was going to have to do that myself. Shit man! I love the arrangements around this house. I thought earlier that I was glad that I had moved here from Cleveland, but shit man, now I know I am more than glad! I'm damn glad in a really big way!"

Then as he looked down at the two strong, long, thick, dicks that Jay and Jake were each hanging, he continued. "Well, let's say I'm damn glad in two big, thick, strong, ways!"

Jake turned to Jay and said, "Think maybe after we eat something, that ass of his will be back to kind of normal, and we can take a couple of more turns on it? How does that sound to you?"

"Shit man!" Jay said. "That sounds damn good to me! Jimmy, can you hang around for awhile after we eat so that my brother and I can get our rocks off in that nice tight ass of yours, again?"

"Oh hell yes, I can!" Jimmy so anxiously answered.

"OK, next question then, man." Jay said. "Can we keep you overnight? Do you have to go anyplace either tonight or tomorrow morning? Can we just kind of keep you here for the rest of the week-end?"

"Oh God men! I was so afraid that after we got this done, that you would then just want me to leave. Oh shit yes man! I can stay! I want to stay! Men, I want both of your cocks up in me and fucking me hard! Yes, men! Yes, please do let me stay, and do fuck my ass some more. OK?"

Jay looked at Jake, and with a big grin on his face said. "Well, brother I sure do hope you have another big load up in you that you need to get out, because it sure does sound to me like we might be fucking, on into Sunday afternoon sometime."

Jimmy then turned toward the two brothers and kind of quietly asked, "Hey guys, in addition to me getting fucked by each of you, I really would like to watch you two fuck each other. I feel really kind of weird telling you guys that, but if that is possible, man that would really excite me. I was kind of afraid that if I was not just straight forward and told you guys that, that it might not happen."

"You're on man!" Jake said to Jimmy. Since I've been out of town a lot lately, Jay and I have not really gotten it on with each other recently, and yeah man, we like to fuck each other, so why not? We've never actually done it as a 'staged performance' for anybody before, but what the hell. You want to watch, you had the guts to tell us that, and we like to fuck each other, so shit yes, we'll fuck for you!"

"Is that OK Jay?"

"Hell yes, it's OK with me. Nobody needs to ask me if I want to fuck in front of an audience. Brother, don't you remember that back alley play they had me in, since I was one of the few guys they could find that was willing to actually fuck a guy on stage in front of an audience? Hey man, yeah – I'll fuck – whatever – wherever – whenever!"

Jake looked at Jimmy and said, "We will discuss that little experience later, OK?"

Jake then took Jimmy out to the laundry room area where they had installed a small bathroom – (shower included), for the convenience of the hidden room – and washed both Jimmy and himself up, and got rid of the grease.

Handing Jimmy a towel, he said. "You can wipe yourself dry with this, but I guess I would suggest that you do not wrap it around yourself to wear upstairs. You heard what Jay said. You will be naked while around here! We'll check the curtains and the blinds, unless you don't mind, anybody and everybody, seeing you run around naked."

"Hey – I'm game!" Jimmy replied, as they headed up the stairs.

Chapter 6

Piece of Pizza, Anyone?

As Jake and Jimmy came up the stairs, Jay was headed back down the hall from the bedroom and bathroom area. "Well, shit man! Sure as hell took you two guys long enough to get yourselves all good and clean. I cleaned up the basement room and came up here and took myself a shower, and you two were still washing down there."

"Yeah, we know!" Jake responded. "Every time you turned on the water up here, we got a real cold bath down there, and had to keep each other warm. Besides, Jimmy just had so damn much grease up in that cute tight little ass of his, that I just had to keep a-washing and a-washing back there to make sure he was all tidy bowl clean. Every time I thought I had him all taken care of, then he'd tell me, 'Sir, I think I might still have a little up over here on this side', and then I'd have to stick my fingers up in there all over again to wash it good and clean. Hell man, his ass must really hold the grease. That happened probably four or five times!"

Grinning widely, Jimmy said. "Well men! You do know that when I visit somebody, I certainly do wish to be a nice clean guest. Having my ass washed and cleaned out by such expert fingers, is the only way to make sure everything is in order!"

"God you are crazy man!" Jay said.

"OK men – supper!" Jay said. "What do we do for food? What time is it? Oh, it's already almost 8:30 already! Damn, time goes by fast when you are having fun!"

"Hey, if it's alright with you two, I could go for a big thick pizza from Pizza Pan tonight if you two are OK with that." Jake said.

"Hell yes! That sounds good to me!" Jay responded. "What about you, Jimmy. How does a pizza sound to you?"

"That sounds great to me! Is the Pizza Pan a delivery pizza place? I've never heard of that place yet."

"Yeah." Jay replied. "It's a privately owned small company. They've got maybe four or five stores in the county. Not a real big company, but I personally think they have the best pizza you can buy anyplace. Eat-in or take out! I mean, buy from either an eat-in place or a take-out place. I'll call and order, but you guys tell me what you want. OK?"

After some light hearted humor about no anchovies and no chitlins, Jay called the Pizza Pan Pantry, to order. During the conversation, Jake and Jimmy heard Jay say, "Who's delivering tonight? Oh, little short Billy? Oh, OK then. Tell him to bring it to the back door. We are back there and we'll be able to hear him better. He's delivered here before. He'll know where to bring it. OK, thanks." And he then hung up.

Jake looked at him in a rather quizzical way and asked. "Bring it to the back door? He will know where that is at. Jay, what in the hell is going on?"

"Oh, I don't have to put any pants on if little Billy is delivering. It happened one night when he walked up right in front of the front window, with the pizza, and I just happened to be walking past the window on the inside. Before I answered the door, I grabbed a pair of shorts and put them on, but then when I opened the door, he said, 'I really wish you had not put those shorts on. I tried to apologize for what had happened, but he told me that he was glad that he walked up right then. Then he told me, 'Instead of you giving me a tip for the delivery tonight, I'd rather just have you take the shorts off again, before I leave'. So now, whenever I know it is little Billy delivering, I don't have to put shorts on. Works out pretty well, don't you think? Fact is he has called here a couple of times and asked me if I wanted a pizza delivered. I'd have to just laugh at him, and tell him thanks for the very personal service, but that I didn't need a pizza that day. You know, I have not had to give him a tip for delivery ever since that one day!"

"Shit man! The stuff that goes on around here when I am out of town!" Jake said. Then turning to Jay, he asked, "So are you and this little Billy getting it on too? Like you and Patrick?"

"No – Billy wants to, but he admitted that he is only 17 right now, so I told him he can look, but no touchy until the night of his 18th birthday, and then I would buy him a pizza and we would have a big birthday party. Just him and me!"

"Uh – so when is the 18th birthday?" Jake asked.

"September the 8th. Not that I remember, but yeah – I do happen to know that I will be busy, that particular night! He is really cute and when he gets here, I think you will see why I am looking forward to September the 8th."

As the three muscular, naked men got the table ready and the drinks prepared, and continued to share some past experiences, the knock on the back door happened.

"Oh here's Billy and the pizza." Jay said. As he started to open the door, he told Jake and Jimmy, "Check him out, guys!"

Jay opened the door, and in complete shock and of course standing there completely naked, he uttered, "Oh My God, you are not Billy!"

"No, I'm Michael!" Michael replied as he looked at the three hunks of beef standing in the kitchen, fully, and so stately, naked.

"But the lady on the phone said that Billy was delivering." Jay rather confusingly said.

"Billy had to leave early today, so he asked me to cover for him. He and I didn't see any reason to tell her that I was covering for him, and right now I am damn glad that we didn't tell her! So, from the instructions to 'deliver to the back door', I assume Billy gets this kind of a treat, each time he delivers here?"

Jake and Jimmy, standing there, completely nude and stunned also, could only grin and smile as Michael started to express a very strong interest in what he had happened to discover – as one of the great treats of delivering pizzas, and Jay's little blunder of sorts.

Taking the pizza from Michael's hand, Jay turned and said, "Just a second. I'll get the money."

Michael, in a very humorous fashion, and with a very large grin on his face, said. "Oh, don't have it in your pants pocket, uh?"

With that remark, Jake asked Michael if he would like to step inside while Jay got the money.

"Yes, I certainly would, if I may. Are you guys having a party or something tonight? Is it the three of you?"

"Well, not really a party." Jake replied. "Just a friendly get together. Of course I'm sure you have already figured out that the other naked guy the one that got us into this rather embarrassing situation, is my brother. He is Jay, I'm Jake, and this is our friend Jimmy."

Michael took a step forward and extended his hand out to shake hands with Jake and Jimmy.

Looking at both Jake and Jimmy, both at their faces and at their exposed dicks, and kind of quickly back and forth from one to the other, he said. "Uh, guys, I get off of work at 11:00 tonight. I don't, kind of think, you guys are going to be just sitting around watching Saturday Night Live, are you? Can I come back right after 11? I can't stay too long, but I sure would like to come back for a few minutes, if I can?"

Looking at Michael with a rather approving smile on his face, Jake asked, "And my dear man, you would like to stop back for what reason?"

"I'd like to get my dick sucked on and get my rocks off!" Michael replied, with his head kind of lowered and rather quietly. "Can I get that done? Would one of you guys do me, if I stopped by for just a few minutes? I've only had that done to me by a guy one time, a long time ago, and I've really been wanting it again lately. I've been trying to find someone for quite awhile now – someone that would do it for me. But I haven't been able to find anybody. Anyway – nobody that I know of. I don't know where to go to find those guys. Does, Billy play when he delivers over here?"

Jay had just returned to the kitchen as he heard Michael ask if he could come back later. "No, he doesn't. He's too young yet." Jay replied to Michael. "But as soon as he has his 18th birthday, then things are going to change." Grinning very wildly, Jay continued. "I'm going to be buying a lot more pizza's from the Pizza Pan Pantry, then!"

With Jimmy just standing there in a complete amassment of the occurrences that were happening, Jake asked Michael, "So, hey, man. You are how old?"

"I'm 19 Sir! Here's my driver's license to prove it."

Jake took the license in his hand and started reading aloud, "Hmm, Michael J. Macenroy, 3866 North Brookshire Lane, apartment B23 – ."

Very, all of a sudden, he was very anxiously interrupted by Jimmy. "What? 3866 North Brookshire Lane?" Looking at Michael he then excitedly asked, "You live in the Brookshire Apartments? That is where I live! What is your apartment number?"

Jake then replied, by looking back down at the license, "B23."

"Shit man! Jimmy exclaimed in surprise. "You live up in the second building in from the street, and I think you drive a little yellow four door car of some kind right?"

"Yeah – yeah. I do and yeah, I've got a yellow Escort."

"Shit man!" Jimmy continued. "I've seen you around there! You've got a wife or a girl friend or somebody else there, right?"

"Uh, I've got a live-in girlfriend. That's Sharon."

"Shit man!" Jimmy explained. "I drive past your building and your parking spot whenever I come in from Brookshire Lane, to get to my place. I've seen you out there before. You have one of those Bar-B-Q pits real close to your apartment, don't you?"

"Yeah, it's kind of right outside our patio door."

"Michael, look at my face. Don't I look familiar to you. You've seen this face before. Maybe not the full naked body, but at least the face! About two weeks ago, I saw you out there by the Bar-B-Q pit in just your gym shorts and no shirt. As soon as I could get my car parked, I went for a walk, just so I could – just kind of – by accident – walk right past your Bar-B-Q area. Your girlfriend was out there with you. I smiled and said, 'Hi' to both of you, and then made some stupid remark that I was hoping you would pick up as a conversation starter. You just said 'Hi', and something about a nice day."

"Jake – Jay! This guy has got one damn hot body under that stupid Pizza Pan plaid costume that he has on, right now. Damn man, he is stacked. He may be delivering pizzas, but shit man, he is really built like a damn beef steak hunk! Hey, Michael, I'm sorry if I'm embarrassing you any, but shit man, if you are wanting a guy to suck you off, you might as well hear what guys think of you! You've got a hot body, man!"

"Yeah – I remember you now. I'm sorry! That was not a good day for me. Sharon and I were in the middle of a fight, and that's why I didn't talk much. I was pissed!"

"Hey Jake – 'Mr. Door Keeper.' Is everything on that license OK, for this guy to stop back later?"

"Looks like he's in for some action later tonight, men." Jake responded.

"Well, about all I can say right now is," remarked Jimmy, "if he is excited at all about coming back later, with those damn loose baggy Pizza Pan pants on, we sure can not tell it. Can we men? Don't you think we ought to ask him to drop the drawers for a second or so, so that we will know what is coming back later?"

"Hell yeah! That sounds good to me." Jay said. "Michael, this may be the first time that a pizza customer has told you to drop 'em guy – but now is the time. Drop them-there-pants, man!"

Taking a very deep breath, Michael obeyed, and dropped his outer pants.

"OK, now, the briefs!" Jay rather ordered.

"Oh shit man! You are right Jimmy. This guy is built! Look at that six pack stomach on him. And look at that flag pole sticking out there." Then looking back at Michael's face, Jay continued. "Are we embarrassing the hell out of you, Michael? I just don't think you get treated this way by a group of guys, very often do you?"

"Yeah, I'm kind of embarrassed, but then all three of you guys are standing there, completely naked, and you are right, I never get treated this way by other guys. Got to admit it though – I like it! I like it a lot! I've been wanting to get to know some guys that I can have some fun with. I like this! So, I can come back right after 11? Right? Please – guys???" Michael very sheepishly pleaded.

"Oh, hell, yes you can man!" Jake said. "But what about your girl friend? Isn't she going to be expecting you home?"

"I'll call her and give her some damn lame excuse of working later or something! I won't be able to stay very long though!"

"Hey, Michael. A good strong, man-on-man blow job don't have to take all night you know! We advertise as "Fast Suck Up Service" here man. We don't do delivery, but we, do – do delivery men!"

Grabbing his pants and pulling them back up, Michael looked at the three hot, all skin shining, meat showing, swinging, and stiff meat sticking out, men, and said, "Guys, I've really got to get going. That other pizza in the van is probably totally cold by now."

Taking just the amount necessary for the pizza, Michael handed back the tip amount to Jay and told him, "Thank you Sir, but I do not need this. I already have been given one big tip today. That was being told to come to the back door. Thank God, Billy left work early! When he has been here before, are all three of you here then, too?"

"No, its been just me, so far.' Jay explained. "Tonight's the first time that these other two have been here when – I thought – Billy was delivering!"

"Shit man!" Michael said. "I really owe him one, for this! Oh, and my second big tip will be later tonight when I come back for a few minutes. I've got to go men! See you later!" Then turning and looking at all three, Michael rather warmly said, "Men, I know this was all an accident today, but I know I will be thanking the heavens for years to come, that this happened. Bye guys, Later!"

"Well!" Jake said. "Now I wonder just how Michael is going to tell Billy about what happened today. Michael has been wanting someone to play with, and I guess as soon as Billy finds out about today's activities, Michael will have a playmate!"

"Shit man!" Jimmy interceded. He will have two! Remember, I just live one building away from that hot little stud, and I intend to keep his ass and his dick as busy as possible. Oh – yeah, I got that girl Sharon to worry about, don't I? Well, maybe I will be able to help Michael decide if he likes meat patties or meat sticks better."

After having some chuckling conversation about what had just happened, and how stuff like that, 'only happens in a porno tape', the three then dug into the pizza and truly enjoyed their first meal together.

Having finished the pizza, Jake looked at the clock and said, "Well men, it is now about a quarter after nine. Michael is coming back here right after eleven. That means we have about one hour and forty five minutes before one of us has the responsibility of giving that poor horny, little straight guy his first blow job in years. Well years – I guess. He said it's been a long time."

Jimmy then added, "Yeah, you assume it's been years, and you are assuming he is a straight guy because he has his live-in girl friend. But, I just about bet you, that give him less than one month of playing around, with either you two guys, or maybe with me, or now, even maybe Billy, and he will finally decide where he is really coming from. No guy is so straight forward as to ask another guy to give him a blow job, when sex has not even been mentioned. Yeah, he was in front of three naked guys, but still, for him to just come out and tell us that he wanted some guy to get his rocks off for him, he knows damn well he is not straight!"

"Yeah, I think I have to agree with you Jimmy! No 'kind of straight guy' is going to be that brazen in front of three guys. Naked or not! If he was really straight, he would be trying to hide his wants and desires, better than that. Shit, he is probably so damn horny for some guy to do him, that he might have asked us even if we had not been naked."

"Yeah – you guys are right!" Jake added. "I just keep thinking all guys know real early in life where they are coming from. I kind of forget that all guys don't have some big, swinging, naked dick brother hanging around them getting them to have sex when they are hardly old enough to know what sex is. Hell, if it wasn't for my horny naked brother, mounting me when we were little, I might not know today if I was straight or not!"

"Don't give me that shit, man!" Was Jay's retort! "You know damn well that you were as horny then as I was, and my naked dick hanging out in front of you had nothing to do with you and your wanting to suck dick! You are the one that kept bringing up the subject every time you had a chance. Sex, Sex, Sex! Hell man! That is all you could think of when Mom and Dad were gone. Man you had your hands on body parts of mine that I did not even know I had!"

"Hey Jimmy, don't pay any attention to either one of us. We do this all the time. We are always trying to convince the other one, or somebody else, that it was the other guy that made the first move! Shit man! I think by the time we finally got to doing it, we were both probably a year behind, in wanting to get it going. If one of us had just come out and said something about a year earlier, then both of us would be walking around with one more year of experience under our belt."

"OK, back to Michael." Jay said. "What's happening there? Are we going to just let him come in here and get a nice polite gentle blow job from one of us, or are we going to give him a true night to remember. Remember guys – do him good, and we just might get some free pizzas out of this!"

"Yeah, right. Free pizzas." Said, Jimmy. "That's not exactly what's on my mind tonight. I still want to watch the two brothers taking care of each other. I'm sorry guys, but that whole idea has had me turned on for so long now, that I just am not going to let it go by. Do I get to watch that before or after Michael is here?"

"Well – " Jake said, rather slowly and thoughtfully. "Let's think this out! Right now my gut is really full from the pizza. What if – what if we kind of just kicked back for a little while, then closer to 11:00 we went down to the basement and one of the two of us, could start working you over Jimmy, while we wait for Michael to show up. That way whichever one is not in your ass, he can come up and get Michael. Oh, shit! I wonder if that room is going to freak Michael out?"

"Hey, no better time to find out than right away!" Jay said. "If we are going to be using him in the future, then he will need to be in that room, so we might as well find out tonight if he can handle that or not."

"Right. Right you are." Jake said. "OK, back to planning. We'll be in the basement. One of us will be in Jimmy's ass. Preferably me, since you, Jay, need to host our pizza guy. When he gets here, then we'll just switch and do some sucking on each other and we'll find out just how many of us take care of poor ole Michael. After he leaves, since I gather he can't stay very long, then we'll get down to some serious fucking for Jimmy's observation. OK, guy? Is that OK with both of you?"

"Yeah, sounds like a plan to me." Jimmy said.

"Yeah, it's OK with me." Jay said. "If you two are already in the playroom when I bring him down, then I'll start on him. Right?"

"Yeah, right Jay. Get him all hot and heavy and see how he reacts. I'm really anxious to see if this is kind of new to him, or does he jump in like he's been doing this before?" Jake replied.

Since the men felt that they had the schedule kind of planned out, they cleaned up the pizza mess in the kitchen and gathered in the living room to watch the evening news, and to just kind of kick back until closer to 11:00.

As Jake went to the living room window to close the curtains, he stopped for a moment and then finished closing them. Jay saw what he was doing, and that he had stopped part way through closing them.

"Hey, Bro. What's up. What you looking at?"

"Well, Jay, I am not sure, but I think I saw somebody over there in that empty field. I think I saw a couple of guys that looked like they were trying to hide. I'm going out back and around the back of the house and kind of peak through the fence to see if that is someone. I'll be right back."

Jake went out the back door and Jay and Jimmy stayed in the living room. Jay then confided in Jimmy and told him, "Yeah, there are guys over there. I've seen them before. I've even checked out that area during the day time, and they've got some boxes over there to sit on and they have them hidden behind a bush. I've seen them watching me a number of times. I figure, hey, if that turns them on, it's OK with me. I don't know who they are, though. I kind of think they are high school boys. I've been trying to figure out how to get them to show themselves. Since that field is the only place that a person can see in here from, I've tried to kind of put on a show for them a couple of times when I've known they are over there. See when they tore that old school building down, that left that big space empty, and the houses on each side of it can't see in this window. Now of course if a person walks down the street, then they can see in. But, hell hardly anybody ever walks down this street, so I don't worry too much about it. Of course Patrick used to, but hell he don't need to anymore."

"What did you do when you said that you kind of put on a show for them?"

"Oh, not too much. I would just kind of walk around the room a little more than usual, and of course my dick would itch, so I'd have to scratch it. I know one time I just happened to be facing the kitchen and I bent over to pick something up. It was after that, that I then stood up and just kind of waved out the window to let them know that I knew they were there, but not bothering me much."

"Hell man." Jimmy injected. "Not bothering you too much in a negative way, but I think they were bothering you in a horny way, right?"

"Oh hell yes, man! If I could have gotten both of them or either one of them to come over here, I would have shown them what good gay sex is all about. I'm still waiting on them to rather appear someday. I know they are wanting it, and I figure that someday, someway, they'll let me know who they are. Until then, it's show time man!"

Jake came back in the back door.

"Yes, Jay. There are a couple of guys over there. I saw them have some small flashlights. I guess since I closed the from curtains, they are not trying to hide as much. I guess the whole reason they are over there is to watch this house. There's no other reason to be in that field!"

"Hey, Jake." Jay said. "Can you tell who they are?"

"No, I couldn't see their faces"

"Could you tell about how old they are? Are they grown men, little kids, teenage boys, like about how old do you think they are?"

"Jay, I really could not tell for sure. In watching them as closely as I could, I think I would guess they're maybe high school age. From the way they moved and walked, I don't think they are grown men."

"Well Jake, why don't you just go over there and ask them who they are. Tell them that your brother has been trying to figure out all summer who they are."

"What? What did you say?" Jake took that statement in shock. "What did you just say? Did you already know they were over there? Jay, how long did you know that? Have you been parading yourself around in front of this window showing yourself off in front of those two guys?"

"Well, kind of. Maybe a little. But it's not always in front of the window. Once I went out front when it was really late and nobody was anyplace close, and I just kind of walked around out there a little so that they would come over here if they wanted to, but I guess they were too afraid. So I don't know who they are."

Looking at Jimmy, Jake then proclaimed. "Shit man! What else am I going to find out about that goes on around here when I am out of town? Shit man! Just since we got to the house this afternoon, I found out that he has been fucking and sucking little Patrick for about a year now. Then I find out that he has Little Billy deliver to the back door so that he can answer it naked and show all his stuff to young little Billy. And now I find out that we have two teenage boys hiding out in the field across the street, and he is in here parading off for them."

Looking at Jay, Jake asks. "Jay, my man. My horny, hung, fucking brother, what else am I going to find out about?"

"Looking up at Jake, Jay replied. "Just that Michael and I have done it before."

"Oh shit man! You are kidding! Right?"

"No, we have hit the hay a few times. He delivered pizzas here one night when Roger and I were here. It happened a lot like tonight, but that time it was for real. Roger and I got him that night after he got off of work. Same thing, 'new' to him. Now Michael just likes to act like it is his first time. He really likes to be told what to do, as if he has never done it. When he gets here tonight, please act like he never gets it. That's his turn on. He really likes for guys to play with him as if this is all new to him. He will actually get pretty 'into' it, but he still likes to act like he has never done this before. It's his game and his fun. So I play along with it. Now don't tell him I told you guys. OK?"

"So I've had this horny gay guy living like about 100 feet from me, and I never knew it? Oh shit, man!' Jimmy said. "Does Sharon know about his activities?"

"I kind of think so." Jay replied. "They seem to have a lot of fights. I kind of think that they might all be over his gay activity. Jimmy, I guess you just might be in the best spot to find out totally what is going on with him. You two guys live close enough, that maybe you can get him to your place a lot, and then see how Sharon handles that."

"OK." Jake then asked. "Once again, let me ask the same question! What else am I going to find out about?"

"Nothing that I can think of right now." Replied Jay. "But hey Brother, can I ask a favor of you?'

"Yeah, I guess. What?"

"Do you mind if we open the curtains up? Those guys like to see us running around nude, and I figure it's no harm done, so why not let them. I'd rather them be over there hiding in the bushes watching us, then out doing something that is going to get them in trouble somewhere."

Then looking at Jimmy, Jay asked. "Is it OK with you if we opened them up?"

Jimmy replied. "Shit man. I think I like running around naked in front of people, well anyway guys, about as much as you do Jay, so that sure is not going to bother me any. Just gets me turned on that much more. It's your house. You do as you wish."

"Jake, may I?"

"Go ahead Jay! If those guys have been hiding out in that field all summer watching over here, I don't see why to stop it now. I will say one thing though! Thank goodness that the playroom is in the basement and that window has been boarded up."

"Oh, Jake." Jay rather softly said. "I kind of forgot to tell you that I fixed that window so the board can be removed. A guy I know likes to watch sex secretly, and so I fixed that window so that I can tell him when to come over and hide outback, and watch me and somebody getting it on together. He can only do that though, when I remove that board. So when I do, I call him and let him know he can watch. It's in the back so I know nobody can see him watching, and the kids across the street can't see in."

"Oh, my God, Jay." Jake exclaimed. "My God Jay! I leave town for a business trip, and all hell comes loose around here. OK, I am going to ask the same question again! What else am I going to find out about?"

"Nothing else. That's it! That's all! I can't even tell you that I got some guy pregnant. Now that would be a hoot wouldn't it?"

Jimmy just kind of sat there and giggled to himself after he checked out Jake's face to make sure all of this stuff was OK with Jake. Both Jay and Jake seemed to be pretty easy going guys, and Jimmy just decided that, especially Jake, had just demonstrated his calm manner. Jimmy looked up at Jake and laughed. Jake looked back at Jimmy and returned the laugh.

"Open the stage curtains, Bro!' Jake said. "Flaunt it good and strong for those guys. Nobody walking down the sidewalk, I hope. Nothing like getting arrested right out of our own house for displaying nudity."

"Hey, when I opened the curtains, I saw those two running, to get behind the bushes." Jay said. "I know they're watching now. When Michael gets here, should I just go across the street and tell them that the show is over for the day?"

"No, Brother, you will do nothing of the kind. If they sit there all night waiting for us to put on another stage show for them, then it's like you said – better there, than off doing something that will get 'em in trouble."

Chapter 7

Yeah-Right – First Time – Sure!

The three horny, naked and hard-on possessed guys rather lost track of the time, as they "attempted" to watch a television program, and at the same time enjoy the naked bodies of each of the other two men on the couch. And their not so shy actions of putting on a slight, man-to-man, performance in front of the window, for the benefit of the two younger, hidden, admirers, watching from in the field, across the street.

The three men heard the knock on the back door, and Jay quickly reminded his brother and Jimmy, "Now guys, remember Michael likes to act like he's never been played with before, so don't let him know that I have told you we played together before, and really treat him like it is his first time with a guy. OK?"

As both of the men replied, "Ok," Jay headed for the kitchen, opened the back door and let Michael in. As they entered the living room, Jay said to Michael, "Hey guy, you remember Jake, the big nasty fucking brother of mine, and Jimmy. We've been kind of anxious for you to get back here. We were all kind of talking about how we are going to take care of you since you have never done this before, so if you've got any questions or anything you want to ask us, now might be the time."

"Uh, no!" Michael replied. "I guess I don't have any questions, but man, looking at those two big cocks you and your brother are swinging, you guys are not planning on fucking me with those things, are you? I know I can not get fucked by you two guys. You will tear my ass all open. Jimmy, have they fucked you before? Do they get up in your ass? Have you ever had one of those big sticks up inside of you?"

"Oh yeah, man!" Jimmy answered. "Yeah, they do Michael, and don't let the enormous size of those two dicks scare you any. It kind of hurts for a moment when they first push it in, but man, your ass is so damn glad they are in there, that after you feel that dick up inside of you, that you beg for more! If you've got a virgin asshole Michael, and either one of them fuck you, you will be wishing you had been doing this for a long time."

"Yeah, but I thought I was just stopping back by here to get my dick sucked on some. You guys have to remember that I'm not a gay guy, and I don't do the things you guys all do. I've never even had a guy's dick in my mouth before, so I don't suck on guys either. Can I just get my dick sucked on by you guys? You won't force me into anything that I don't think I should be doing, will you?"

"Oh no Michael!" Jay replied. "No man! You can be sure we will not be doing anything or making you do anything that you don't think you should be doing. We'll take care of you. Come on, let's go to the basement and get started on that dick of yours since you said that you won't have too much time before you need to get home to your woman.

"Yeah, it's already about 11:30 and I can't stay out too much longer. I'll need to get home pretty soon or she will be asking me where I was at after work."

Jay turned toward the front window and make a quick wave. He knew the two young guys were watching from across the street. He rather liked letting them know that he knew they were there. He liked the feeling that he just knew they got all excited knowing that he, their visual subject, knew he was being watched, and was kind of playing along with them.

The four men, three completely nude, and the newcomer, Michael, headed for the basement.

As they got to the basement, Michael said, "Now guys, you've got to remember this is all new to me and I don't know what to do. You are going to have to tell me what I am supposed to do, but please, no funny stuff with me. OK?"

"Oh no, man!" Jay answered. "No funny stuff at all Michael. First thing is though, we can't do you if you are going to stand there all completely dressed. Get those clothes off so we can see the damn big stick you showed us earlier."

Michael took his shirt and pants off, and finally after getting his socks off, stood before the three men completely nude and showing all of his hot structure to his late night playmates.

"Hot – right men?" Jay asked.

"Right!" Jimmy replied. "I'm glad to get to see this all bare and naked. Once I realized that he was the same guy as the one at the apartment complex, I've been really anxious to see the whole thing. Oh, look guys! As we stand here and look at the merchandise, it is getting all excited. Tell you what guys. We need to get some organization going here so that we are all getting what we want. Why don't I get myself down here in front of this big white stick, that is now pointing up at us, and while I suck on it for a little while, one of you two start sucking on your brother and then Michael can watch a guy suck on another guy, while he is getting sucked on too."

"Yeah, sounds like a plan to me!" Jay said. "Jake, on your knees brother, I need my dickie sucked on. And while you are doing me, I'll watch Jimmy do Michael and then later we will shift and make some changes. From the looks in this room tonight, there are four really good sized dicks and I think all of them need some attention. Suck me brother!"

Jake did not object to his brother's instruction. Jake immediately knelt down in front of his twin's crotch and without even touching Jay's dick, slid his mouth down onto it, and pushed his head forward hard enough to take the entire length of Jay's cock down into his throat.

Michael was watching and exclaimed. "Oh my God! Oh man! You took his whole damn dick like that? You just pushed it down without any gagging? Oh shit man! Oh man, how in the hell can you get that much cock down your throat so fast?"

Jimmy knew that Michael's watching Jay's dick go down Jake's throat so fast was a complete turn on to him. As Michael watched, his own dick, completely sunken into Jimmy's mouth, gained a sudden spurt in size and stiffness. Jimmy knew Michael was getting very excited. As Michael's dick continued to harden, it also continued to grow. Jimmy worked his mouth on it with good strong motions and clamping actions. Michael grabbed ahold of the back of Jimmy's head and started using Jimmy's head as a jerk-off tool for his own personal pleasure. He was jerking Jimmy's head back and forth as if it was simply one very big hand that was jerking him off.

Jake was very slowly moving on and off of his brother's dick. He was enjoying the warm full feeling that Jay's dick was giving to him. Jake did not feel the necessity of making sure his brother came as quickly as possible. He knew that he would have all of the time he needed to get his brother to a – "shooting off sensation!" Jake had filled his mouth with his brother's cum many times before, and he realized that giving Jay the time to really build up a complete load, simply made the explosion action that much more exciting for both of them. From prior experiences, Jake had learned that sucking on Jay in a very caring and loving way, was a much more exciting experience than to force him into a quick and early climax. Jake had a firm grip on Jay's butt cheeks so that the could pull his brother in toward himself and then back away from himself, so that he could maintain a good solid position in his kneeling position. Jay enjoyed the motion that his body was forced into doing, due to his brother's strong arm motions, and his strong hand grips onto his butt. Jay closed his eyes, turned his head upward, and at the some time reached down and took ahold of his brother's tits with a thumb and a finger of each hand.

As Jay's hands grabbed slightly ahold of Jake's tits, Jake, uttered a quiet moan of pleasure. The two brother's were actually loving each other at this moment in time. They had moved beyond just having sex together. Jake's control of Jay's standing body, and in return, Jay's gentle but firm grip on each of Jake's tits were more than just having sex. Each man was silently expressing a true love for the man that he had control over, and that man was his identical twin.

Jimmy had gained a glimpse of the actions going on beside himself, and realized that a suck off was not the important item happening beside him. This in turn, resulted in Jimmy's increasing love of, and for the dick that was currently using his mouth as a jerk off tool. Although Jimmy had pretty well lost control of how he performed on Michael, he did have a very strong feeling of love move though himself. He felt as if it actually moved through and from his body, out though his skin, and into the man what was face fucking him right then. Although he realized that he hardly knew Michael, all of a sudden he felt a very, very strong attraction to this man, and felt that maybe he had known Michael in, some, "former life." He suddenly became very, very attracted to Michael. He grabbed Michael by the butt muscles and forced his face up against Michael's stomach and refused to allow it to be pushed back. He swallowed Michael's cock as deeply down, into, his throat, as far as it would go, and mentally caressed and made love to the tip of that cock, with the lining of his throat. Unexplainably, he completely fell in love with Michael's entire body. Jimmy anxiously ran his hands up and down the sides of Michael's body, up and down the inside and outside of Michael's legs, and then ran his left hand up across Michael's chest as his right hand reached up and caressed Michael's back.

Michael sensed that something rather different and weird was happening. He knew that Jimmy's actions had changed dramatically. He did not attempt to move Jimmy's head, he allowed Jimmy to push it into his stomach as strongly and as firmly as Jimmy could manage. Michael was receiving this unexplained feeling of love. He realized it was a love, and he also realized that it was being transferred from a man that he had only known for probably 30 minutes or less, total time. He liked the feeling, and he accepted it graciously. He felt that he and Jimmy were truly experiencing an unexplained emotion that seldom happens, and certainly never between two men that do not yet know each other.

Michael slightly loosened his hands on Jimmy's head, as if to say something like, "You take control now man."

Jimmy pulled his head back, and after removing his mouth from around Michael's man stick, he looked up at Michael and quickly said. "Babe, shoot everything you've got into my mouth, and then just as soon as you do, lay down on the mat, on your stomach. OK?"

"Yeah, yes, hon." Michael replied. The 'Babe' and the 'Hon' were never questioned by either man. Those terms were automatic and felt very normal.

Jimmy replaced his mouth onto Michael's cock and indicated by his body motions that it was time for Michael to fill his mouth with his warm white liquid juices.

Michael had heard the instruction to fill his man's mouth with everything that he had, and to then lay down on the mat, on his stomach. He did not understand this instruction, but had no second thought of even attempting to ask why, or even ponder just what was going to happen when he did that.

Ever so lovingly Michael fucked Jimmy's mouth, and every so lovingly Jimmy allowed his face to be fucked.

Michael's body started to straighten up, and his dick got even harder and stiffer than it had been earlier. Jimmy grabbed ahold of

Michael's butt muscles and attempted some sound of something like, "Yeah, do it, do it!" or something that allowed all three men in the room to know that Jimmy was begging for all and everything, that was just about ready to be shot into him.

Jake and Jay were still in the mode of sucking and being sucked, but without anybody saying anything other than Jimmy's instructions to Michael, they had each sensed that something rather 'different' was happening between the two men beside them. They continued their own personal actions, but at the same time, each man, kept an eye open to see what was going to be happening next.

As Michael's body straightened up and became rigid, he grabbed Jimmy's head and pulled it into his crotch and lowly yelled, "Oh, man! I'm cumming man! I'm cummin' man – I'm cumming! Oh Jimmy, I'm cumming!"

Jimmy attempted to utter, "OK, OK," but had his voice restricted with the mouth full of man cum that was filling his entire mouth.

Michael humped his torso toward, and into, Jimmy a couple of times, and Jimmy continued his clamp onto Michael's flowing dick. As soon as Jimmy realized that Michael had finally stopped shooting more and more fluids into his mouth, Jimmy gently started to turn Michael around as if to remind him that he was to immediately lay down on the mat, with his butt up.

Michael immediately hit the mat. He was still confused about what was happening and why he was to do this, but he had no desire to make any question. He looked at Jimmy and realized that Jimmy still had his mouth full of cum clamped tightly into his mouth.

As Michael's stomach hit the mat, Jimmy's face landed squarely and firmly in Michael's ass crevice. Michael felt Jimmy's tongue approach his asshole. Slowly Jimmy's tongue forced Michael's rectum hole to open. With one forceful motion, Michael felt Jimmy's mouth get pressed up tightly, between his ass cheeks, up firmly against his asshole, and all of a sudden, a flow of warm fluids being blown up, into his ass. Michael immediately knew that he had just taken back, his own load of cum that he had just given to Jimmy!

"Lay still honey, I'm about to fuck you!" Jimmy said. "You've already been lubed up, and now I'm coming in! So lay real still!"

Michael did not plead against it. He did not seem to be playing his normal roll of acting like this was his first time of ever doing anything like this. Michael did not say anything! Realizing what Jay had told them earlier, Jimmy really did not know if Michael had actually ever been fucked before or not, but he decided that if he truly had never been before, tonight would be his first.

Jimmy was completely ready in the "having a good, stiff, strong hard-on ready" area. As he removed his face from Michael's ass, he moved up and immediately positioned his dick head at Michael's asshole. He listened for any comment about how they could not do this, but none was uttered.

Jimmy started lowering his body down onto, and his cock into Michael. Michael made one rather slight re-positioning motion, seeming to get himself into a more acceptable position for the big dick that was in the process of entering his body, but other than that, made no suggestion that this should not be happening. He did, in-fact, lowly and kind of quietly, but emphatically, plead, "Oh Hon, fuck me please!"

When Jimmy heard that, he knew everything was going to be OK. He slowly but gently continued to push his stiff and hardened stick up into Michael's body. He knew there had to be a little bit of pain. He did not feel like the cum job, that he had spit back into Michael's hole, had done a complete job of lubricating Michael's entire asshole. He listened closely for any comments coming from Michael that this was not working. Michael only made some body motions and movements, but never said anything that Jimmy took as an indication that he needed to stop.

After Jimmy got his entire eight inches or so, imbedded into Michael's ass as far as possible, he created as much forceful pressure on Michael's body as he could. He pushed and enjoyed the body to body contact that he was experiencing.

After taking a rather deep breath, Michael said. "Oh man! That feels so good in me! Hon, I've never been fucked before. I've never had a dick up in me before. Oh man! Damn, man that feels so damn good! Please move it around in me so I can feel it up in there, please. Yeah – yeah – oh man – oh man – oh that is so damn good! Oh God, Jimmy! You feel so good up in me!!!!!!! Fuck my ass please! Please let me know what it is really like to really, really get fucked, please man! Please, I've got to feel all of you up in me!"

Jimmy was using his new playmate to his full and complete pleasure. He had his cock rammed up in Michael's ass as far and as forcefully as he could get it. He turned toward Jay and Jake and gave them a big grin. They understood that he was using this new toy boy to his complete enjoyment.

"So," Jimmy asked Michael. "So you have never been fucked before, huh?"

"No, I have never been fucked. Really! I've sucked on guys before and I've been sucked off before, but I've never been fucked. I was afraid to do that, and tonight I just decided that I had to get it." Michael answered. "Yeah, I know I told you guys that I have never played around at all before, and I figured Jay told you to just play along because he knew that was what I liked to do, and if we were just sucking, then I would have continued that line, but oh, Jimmy, now that you are in my ass and it feels so damn good. I've got to be straight with you guys and admit that yes, I've sucked on guys and been sucked on too, but no, tonight is the very first time that I have ever let a guy put his dick up in my ass. When I played with Jay and his buddy before, the size of his dick just plain scared the hell out of me too much. The way you are making me and my ass feel right now, I can't lie. I can't play that stupid game anymore. I just can't let you think that you are playing with something different than what I really am. Now that I've finally let a guy put his dick up in me, I want you to get really wild with me! Now I know there wasn't any reason for me to be so afraid of this. Fuck me Jimmy, and fuck me damn, real damn hard! Please! I've been trying to get the nerve up to getting my ass fucked for a long time now, and finally tonight I got the nerve up to get it done to me, and so now I want it hard, now that I know I can do it. I want to be a real man! I want you to make me be a real man! Fuck me man! Please fuck me! Really fuck me please! I've been wanting this done to my ass for a long time."

"OK man, I'm willing and I'm anxious to do what you want. I'm going to fuck your ass like crazy. You are asking for it, you are telling me that you want to be made a real man tonight, and you are acting like you really do want it, so I am going to really fuck you! Hang on man, here we go! I just hope you know what you are asking for, because you are going to get a real good hard fucking!"

With that statement, Jimmy started in on Michael's asshole like he had not fucked any guy in a long time. He had Michael's body actually bouncing up and down on the floor. Michael kept yelling for, "More – harder man! Do me harder! Harder, harder!"

"Shit man, I'm fucking you as hard and as fast as I can!" Jimmy told Michael. For more that ten minutes, Jimmy pounded Michael's ass with his man stick dick as fast and as hard as he could. Finally, completely out of breath and in exhaustion, Jimmy all of a sudden stopped, and laid down on Michael's back.

"God! Shit Man!" Jimmy managed to say. "My God Michael, your ass should be screaming in pain right now. I have fucked you harder than if you had gotten fucked by some crazy mountain lion or some fucking elephant bull. Shit man, I'm worn out!"

Jimmy laid across Michael and attempted to catch his breath. He had exhausted himself trying to give Michael more ass end fucking than he could take. He told Michael what he had tried to do, then continued, "I failed man! Shit, man, I was trying to get you to beg off and ask me to stop, but shit man, your ass can take an 18 wheeler right now, I think! Jay, Jake, I need to rest for a minute, why don't one of you come over here and fuck this ass and see if one of you can get him to holler, 'Uncle'."

"Yeah! I will!" Jake said. "That ass needs a good long thick black stick in it and I'm the one to do it. Jimmy, roll off of him and let me at that ass! I'm going to help make him the real man, that he said he wants to be! He's going to think he just got fucked by some big ole horse!"

Jake mounted Michael and immediately rammed his entire length up into Michael's ass. Michael made one low groan as Jake's steak stick hit the bottom of Michael's ass chamber, and then following that one low moan started begging Jake to fuck him rough and hard.

"Please man! Please harder! Yeah, man! Please fuck me hard, do me harder!"

Jimmy looked over at Jay and asked. "So you guys have never fucked together, right? You have never fucked this guy before, right?"

"Well, no, we haven't! We have played around together but he never got fucked before. He kind of always, kind of acted like maybe he wanted to, but then would always say no. I mean yeah, I kind of thought he always wanted to, but I've never seen him get fucked, and if this really is his very first time, shit man, he is really into it! I'm going to let Jake use him for just awhile, then I am going to fuck him too! Man, by the time he is out of here tonight, he is going to know he got fucked. He is going to know he got fucked big time! He may not remember just where in the hell he was, and he may not be able to walk, but by God he will know he got fucked. Jimmy, I have to admit that I have never been with any guy that is as hungry for getting his ass done as rough as he is tonight! I can't hardly believe that he has never been fucked before. Especially since he is so damn anxious for it, and wants it so damn rough. His ass is way hungry, man! I've played with a lot of virgin asses in my time, but man, I have never ever been with a new ass that is this damn hungry! He sure as in hell has lost his ass fucking fear, real quickly!"

"Well, all I know is that even with the rough fucking I did to him, I did not cum and if you are going to fuck him after Jake gets done, then he is going to get at least four fuckings tonight because I am going to fuck him again so I can load his ass with some of this Jimmy juice!"

Jimmy and Jay watched Jake do Michael's ass as rough, as fast and as hard as Jake could manage. The entire time that Michael was getting fucked, he continued to beg and plead for more, rougher, harder! He kept yelling, "Fuck me man! Fuck me man!"

Jake was sweating and breathing heavily when he finally let out a quick groan of, "Oh shit man! I'm cummin man! I'm cummmin'!" His entire body stiffened up and Jimmy and Jay could see him pushing into Michael's ass as he unloaded, what must have been a complete bag full, and then a complete, ass full of cum. He continued to pump and hump on Michael's ass as he kept groaning that "I'm coming, I'm coming!" Finally he collapsed on top of Michael and his entire body went limp.

Jay quickly told his brother to move. "This guy is still begging for more dick and I am the next one to give it to him. Let me in his ass. Michael my man, get ready! I'm going to fuck you crazy!"

"Good, good! Fuck me man! Fuck me hard! Fuck my ass!"

Jay mounted Michael's ass and rammed his black meat stick into Michael's ass as quickly as Jake had done. Slam bang, it was in! Michael again kind of groaned as it hit rock bottom in his ass chamber. Once again, he kept begging for a good hard rough fucking. He was acting like was so used to getting fucked like that and he certainly was not acting like this was the very first time a guy had ever been up in his ass.

Now it was Jake and Jimmy that were sitting along side of this unbelievable fucking session, shaking their heads in disbelief of how much fucking and abuse Michael was begging for, and was actually taking from all three of this guys.

"Shit man!" Jake said. "I heard Jay tell you that he has never been with a guy that can take this much action in his ass, and I have never either. Man, I can not believe the abuse that asshole is taking tonight! Your dick is not small Jimmy, but my God man. Jay and I do have really, really big dicks for going up in a guy's ass, and most guys get real scared about taking them up in their asses. And this guy, I kind of think would take both of them at once if we told him that is what we are going to do to him. I don't think he would object at all! You are going to re-fuck him again, so you can load him up, right??"

"Yeah, I sure plan on it" Jimmy said. "That is if he will let me back in there after you and Jay get done with him. Shit man, I watched you go to hell on him, and my ass was hurting just watching you pound it like you did, and now Jay is doing the same damn thing. Man! Is he going to be able to stand up when we are done with him?"

"I don't know Jimmy! Jay and I watched you pound the fucking hell out of his ass when you were fucking him, and we both were amassed at the treatment he was taking from you, then I got on him and tried my best to wear him out, now Jay is acting like some untamed wild fucking animal on him, and he is still begging for more. And this is the guy that was supposed to act like he had never had gay sex before? Shit man! I really do wonder if this really is his first time getting it up the ass. I know I sure as the hell love to get it in the ass good and rough, but shit man, I've never seen any guy take it like he is tonight! Do you really thing this is his first time?"

"I don't know." Replied Jimmy. "But I will tell you that I want to be involved again, if he can take it this fast and furious all of the time."

Jay was slamming Michael's ass at least as hard if not harder than the two previous guys that had been fucking Michael, and yet Michael was still begging for more! As Jay humped and slammed Michael's ass, he was starting to show some wear and tear. He was breathing heavy and was sweating heavy from his forehead. He fucked Michael's butt hole for a good 10 to 15 minutes without giving up. It rather seemed that everybody in the basement room that night was determined to be the winner. All three tops had tried their very best in getting Michael to beg off of getting any more dick up his ass, and trying to find out what his limit was. Michael himself seemed to be in a challenge of letting all three men do their thing to him, for as long and as hard as they wished, without him asking for a break. So far, Michael was turning out to be the winner.

Jay reacted very much like his twin brother. He was in fast action fucking motion, going at Michael's ass as strong and as hard as he could, when all of a sudden, his body completely tightened up, his whole body went stiff, he pushed hard on Michael's butt, his dick pushed into Michael's ass as far as it could go, and he let out a load moan, of – "Oh, man, I'm cumming – I'm cumming! Oh shit man! Oh shit! Oh shit man! I'm cummmming man – I'm cumming!" He was louder than Jake had been and almost screamed it.

Jake looked at Jay and told him to "Whoa man! Not so loud! We do have neighbors you know. You don't need to be telling them what you're doing down here! That little old lady next door – she might come a-running if she heard you yelling that!"

Jay and Jimmy rather laughed at that comment. Jimmy was doing OK, but Jay was definitely out of breath, and as far as Michael went, he was still laying there on the mat and kind of crying in a low and pleading tone, "Please, please, please! Please men, please somebody fuck me!"

"Oh my God!" Jimmy exclaimed! "My God man! He is actually begging for more dick. His ass should be raw! Damn! I have not shot off yet and I said that I was going to re-fuck him, but I really thought that by the time you two railroad car dicks got out of him he would be begging for everything to stop. Shit man, he still wants it! I can't believe he is taking it like this! I've got it and he is going to get it!"

And with that statement, Jimmy remounted Michael's ass. Once again Michael took the entering dick without so much as new lube and definitely without so much as a statement to him that he was about to get entered. His ass was open, ready and anxious!

As Jimmy started pounding Michael's ass, he looked over at Jay and Jake and said. "Men, we have got to get this guy on tape. We've got to do a tape of him getting fucked by probably about ten or twelve guys. This guy could probably get fucked by twelve guys – one right after the other, and still be begging for more! I've never seen a guy with an ass this hungry!! We need to do a tape so that everybody can tell there was no editing, and that this guy just takes it and takes it, and takes it!"

Jay and Jake looked at each other, and without saying anything, gave each other a look of, "Well – yeah maybe that is a good idea." They each then kind of shook their heads as if to say, yeah, maybe so.

Jimmy had gotten himself up to speed while mentioning the tape idea, and was now fucking Michael's ass as roughly as he had done earlier and was trying to match the speed and roughness that Jay and Jake had used on Michael while they were each fucking him.

Michael continued to ask for more, and continued to beg for harder – rougher. Jimmy was doing his best at complying with the requests. He was using Michael's ass like he had never done to any guy before. He had decided that if this guy can beg and plead for more, rougher, deeper, harder after he has been fucked four times already, and all within the last hour, then he was going to give everything, that he had in him, to this hungry ass.

Jimmy fucked Michael, rough, hard, slamming, and jamming as well as slow and calmly for some time periods, so as to be able to recoup his breath and get ready for the next go at it.

Jay realized after a short period of time that Jimmy was going to be enjoying this ass fucking session for some time, and he was not going to hurry though this one. He turned to his brother and said, "Well Bro. Jimmy asked us earlier today if we would fuck for him, and since it looks like he is going to be doing Michael's ass for awhile, why don't we get ourselves positioned over here where he can watch us, while he takes care of Michael's ass. I'll fuck you, and then he can fuck and watch us, all at the same time."

"Good – sounds good to me. So I guess it has already been decided that you are the one on top tonight, right?"

"Right! Right you are man! Tonight I fuck your ass. If you will remember right, the last three times that we have been in bed together, you were the top. Always something about since you were going to be out of town, you needed to get your rocks off so that you did not try to hump every good looking guy you saw. So tonight, it's my fucking turn. Oh! No pun intended on the term, "fucking turn" but yes – it is my fucking turn! Lay your butt down there brother, you are about to get fucked!"

Jimmy looked over at the brothers and said, "Good men! Man this is going to be hot! I get to watch you two hot built, black men, identical twin fuckers, fucking each other, while I get my jollies off over here, on this one. What could be better! Maybe we can fuck in rhythm!"

With that remark, Jay and Jake laughed and proceeded to get in their fucking position beside Jimmy and Michael. As he mounted his brother's ass, Jay rubbed some lube on his dick and some on Jake's ass. He slowly raised his mid section up so that his dick was immediately above Jake's asshole. Holding his cock with his left hand and guiding it into place, Jay slowly lowered himself down onto, and into, his brother. Jake made a low moan of pleasure as he felt his brother's thick stiff ten inch cock slide into his innards. He adjusted his position ever so slightly, and enough for Jimmy to know that Jake's insides were feeling full. Jimmy had just recently had that same big dick up in his ass, and so he fully knew what a full ass feels like. Mentally he thought, 'Oh man! I fucking know that feels just about like sitting down on top of a steel fence post, and letting that stiff ole post go on up, and inside of your ass!'

As Jimmy continued to fuck Michael's ass, he watched as the two beautiful, muscular, shapely, structured, mahogany toned, body builder, identical brothers made love to each other. Jimmy liked the way it was hard to tell exactly where one body quit and the other began. Both men were so identical looking, that Jimmy realized that if they had gotten into this sexual position without him knowing which one was going to be doing the fucking and which one was going to be the one getting fucked, he would have had trouble telling which one, was which.

The sight of these two gorgeous men making love to each other was outstanding to Jimmy. Then, for him to realize that these two unbelievable specimens were brothers and they could so lovingly have sex with each other was way too much for Jimmy to imagine! Beautiful he thought! Just plain damn beautiful! He watched as Jay lovingly slid his tongue along the neck line of his brother. He watched as Jay so very carefully and lovingly ran his hands down along the side of his brother's torso. He recognized that Jay's touch was a very magic touch to his brother. He could tell that they were experiencing an exchange of, maybe electrodes or whatever it is when it is an exchange that can not be seen or identified. Jimmy just knew that as twins, they had the unexplainable power of feeling what the other person also feels, and even in this moment of love and caring, the other brother simply knew what his brother was feeling, and he was feeling it all back to himself too. Jay was so gently giving to his brother some very deep and caring emotional touching that was being passed back to the giver in a very strange and unexplainable way. Jimmy felt that he had never, in his entire life, ever had the opportunity to witness such a sharing and a giving of true love between two human beings.

As Jimmy continued to fuck Michael, he would often ask Michael to look at the brothers and share with him the beautiful feelings that the two black brothers were sending out from their space in the room. Often Jimmy would ask Michael, "Oh, Michael, isn't that beautiful. Look at the way Jay is treating his brother's body! Look at the way he is loving that human mass of flesh that he is laying on. Michael, just imagine – one brother is so lovingly inside of the ass of his own brother, and they are both in such complete joy over it! Oh, Michael, isn't that beautiful?"

Jay overheard Jimmy's comments to Michael more than once, and each time he would look over to the two new friends, fucking right beside them, and he would give his brother an extra long hug, or perhaps run his hand down the entire length of Jake's beautiful muscular strong body. Although the two men were still very identical, and both possessed almost completely perfect bodies, Jay did worship Jake's body as Jake did back to Jay, when he was the top, fucking, brother. The two steel strong men once again had the opportunity to let somebody else realize their admiration for each other, as they had about two years earlier, when they were pictured on the cover of a local gay magazine, devoted to 'special gay people." Only this time it was a little more personal, and some true moving action could be shown and demonstrated. They did not have to be just still shots this time. This was much more exciting to them. They were, and could act like true living human beings. Not just perfect bodies with perfect poses. This time they could actually let the "reader" know that – yes, they do fuck each other. When the magazine was published, they wanted it stated that yes, they do have sex with each other, but the publisher refused to include that, and rather portrayed them as being just two gay, but very handsome and very well structured, black brothers, that got along.

Jimmy and Jay started watching each other. They started imitating whatever action the other person was doing. As one fucker got faster, so did the other. If one slowed down, so did the other. This playing around was 'just between them.' Their bottom partners did not realize what was happening. Jimmy and Jay were not only fucking their sex partners, but they were also enjoying the comrade between themselves too.

Jimmy had, for some unknown reason, become the leader of this, 'do as I do action'. He started fucking Michael faster and faster.

He was returning back to the type of fucking that had been going on earlier in Michael's ass. As he got faster, and faster, so did Jay. Soon, they were acting as if they were involved in a high speed road race. Each man was attempting to out do the other person. They had very happy bottoms, although Jake and Michael were not aware they were involved in a race. They each just thought their top man had gotten himself all excited and was really going after the ass he was in. Little did they know, they had actually become somewhat of a race car! Being ridden and driven very fast and very rough. Of course for Michael, this was just what he was still wanting. He was still begging for 'more, faster, harder, rougher'.

As the two tops gained speed and action, Jimmy realized that he was starting to get real ready and real close to a climax, and he looked over and kind of quietly asked Jay if he was getting ready too. Jay told him yes, he was getting really, really, close.

"Good!" Jimmy replied. "Keep looking toward me so I can tell how close you are getting. I want us to cum at the same time."

The two men started watching each other very closely so that they could time their climaxing together. All of a sudden Jay let out a large and loud, "Now!"

Jimmy came back with a sudden and loud, "I'm shooting man, I'm shooting! Oh God yes man – I'm shooting! I'm shooting it man – I'm shooting it!"

Jay yelled, "I am too! I am too! God I am too! I am too! Load your man! Load your man! Oh yeah do it, do it, do it!"

Each man shot his wad and grabbed his partner as he pushed his man stick up in him as far as it could go, for one last surge of white cum up into his partner's ass. They then each collapsed on their bottom's backsides.

Exhausted, Jay looked over at Jimmy and said, "Pretty damn good racing, wouldn't you say, guy?"

"Yeah, yes and right on!" Jimmy replied.

"What in the hell are you two talking about?" Jake asked.

"Oh, you and Michael didn't know it, but you two were kind of our race horses or race cars or something. Jimmy and I were having our own little race event up here using you two guys, and your asses. I think we came in as a dead heat. No winner. No – wait! Yes – I think all four of us are winners! You know what? Especially Michael! Do you know that guy got cum loads from four different guys up in his ass tonight?

"What?" Jake asked. "What do you mean?"

"Well, you loaded his ass once. I loaded his ass once. Jimmy loaded his ass once. And he loaded his own ass earlier when he shot it in Jimmy's mouth, and Jimmy gave it back to him, up in his ass. So – see, he's gotten four loads from four different guys tonight!

"He's one hell of a fucking pizza delivery guy, isn't he?" Jimmy laughed. "I just wonder how many customers he gives this type of delivery service to in a day! What are we going to do with him now? He's lying there like he is all exhausted now. He sure does not look like he is too anxious to get home to that girl friend of his, does he? I kind of guess she's never quite been able to give him the same type of loving that he has gotten here tonight."

Jake looked at Jay and said, "Well man. We sure do have enough room around here for more that just one house guest tonight, don't we? What do you think?"

Jay replied. "Why not? I'm not so sure he can get up off of that floor right now anyway."

Michael looked up at the three men, smiled, and mouthed, "Thank you, thank you!" He then laid his head back down on the mat and quietly said, "I need to get fucked!"

Chapter 8

Quite a Day, Isn't It?

Jay slowly woke up realizing that he was being brought to life on this "early" Sunday morning by having his very muscular, tight, firm, mahogany toned skin, kissed and licked on. As he opened his eyes so slightly, he looked down to see Jimmy so very gently kissing and chewing on his left nipple.

Jay slightly repositioned himself so that he would be in a much better position for Jimmy to so lovingly caress his master of a hunk, bodybuilder's body and tits, with his mouth. Jay smiled, and reached down and softly placed his hand on the back of Jimmy's head. Jimmy looked up at Jay's face and although he had a mouth full of brown mahogany muscles in his mouth, he did manager to smile back.

Jake turned his head toward his twin brother and smiled. He very quietly told Jay, "Hey brother, I kind of think you and I have just found out the proper way to be wakened up in the morning."

Jay replied, "So right brother, so damn right!"

Michael was attending to Jake's body with the same care and compassion as his friend Jimmy was doing to Jay. Both white men, the younger two of the foursome, continued their respective journeys along all lines of the two beautiful twin brothers that they had just become friends with. Each man, the two younger white guys, worshipped and kissed the bodies of the two muscle men that carried the body structures that they, each knew in their hearts, they would love to look like someday, but each knew that nature just was not going to be on their side – in gaining that much masculinity – that much "he-man strength" – nor that much machismo, as these two beautiful brothers had managed to gain. Gained – either through natural forces, or through hundreds of hours pushing and pulling iron in the gym. Michael and Jimmy were each experiencing some very silent loving and admiration of some human male bodies that, to them, really could not be real humans. The two specimen lying beside them were just too perfect to be real. Each man realized that if this was truly a dream, and that they would eventually wake up and realize it had all been a dream – simply an imagination within their own heads, then damn it – while they were in their dream land, they were going to enjoy every small lick, every small nibble, every small hug and every small thought of it!

As Jimmy continued to lick and kiss Jay's body, an identical action was happening between Michael and Jake. The two hosting brothers simply laid back and offered their respective bodies, to each of the two young men that was so lovingly worshipping their respective muscle man.

When Michael started to reach just a little too low on Jake's torso, Jake rather laughed and while raising his head told Michael, "Oh, hey man. Better not go there right now! I'm really needing to go take a piss, and I'm afraid that if you touch it, you might get something that kind of looks like Niagara Falls, falling all over you face!"

Michael looked up at Jake's face and with a laugh said. "OK man, I understand. Go take a piss man! Jimmy and I kind of started taking advantage of you two guys before you even woke up this morning, so maybe we had better leave you guys alone for a little while and not get our asses thrown out of here for being too pushy!"

"Hell, man! You ain't being too pushy at all!" Jake replied. "I do have to go take a piss, but don't you ever think that I do not appreciate getting woken up in the morning like this. Shit man, when you live with something like my brother here, all I ever get woken up with – is some yelling about why I need to get my fat ass out of bed and do something! It's kind of nice to wake up with a nice warm mouth, running up and down your body."

"Fat ass?" Jimmy quickly asked. "Fat ass? I certainly do hope he was using that just as a comment and did not mean it. Shit man, if that is what a guy calls a fat ass, I'd sure hate to see a skinny muscular ass. If he calls your ass a fat ass, I guess he has to realize his ass is identical!"

"Oh yeah! He does." Jake answered as he got up from the mat and headed for the bathroom. "You've got to remember, I have a brother that never likes to say nice things about me, even though most of the time I'm the nicer guy." With that remark, he grinned from ear to ear and headed out the door.

Jimmy had released his hold on Jay and was now laying beside him on the mat, with Michael laying on his other side.

"So what time did you two guys wake up?" Jay asked the two visitors.

"Well, time wise, I'm not sure. I'm not even too sure what time it is right now. But we were awake probably half an hour or forty five minutes before we attached you two. We woke up, we each noticed that the other guy was awake too, but realized that you two were still pretty well conked out. So anyway, being the nice guys that we are, we kind of played with each other for a little while, and then when you two kind of rolled over and were not right up against each other, we very quietly, almost using hand signals, decided to each take a man, and help that man wake up. So anyway, instead of using something like an alarm clock, we decided to lick you awake. And it worked."

"Damn right it worked! And what a beautiful way to wake up! It felt damn good guys!"

Jake re-enter the playroom and proclaimed. "Damn man! That feels better! Anybody else in here got to go take an early morning piss?"

Michael and Jimmy both admitted that yes, they each needed to go pee, as Jay looked over at his brother and asked. "Hey man – early morning piss – I don't even know what time it is. What time is it? Is that clock still over there on the shelf?"

"Oh shit man! It's 10:00 already! Shit man! I had no idea it was that late. This basement is so damn dark with that window boarded up. I guess maybe we should have taken that cover off of that window last night before we went to sleep so that some daylight could come in this morning!"

"If I kind of remember last night correctly at all, I kind of think the very last thing that we were worried about was light in the morning." Jay replied. "We had a guy down here that just could not get enough, and our minds were on that, a hell of a lot more, than on morning light. Which, by the way Michael, how does you ass feel this morning? Is it OK?"

"Yeah, it's fine! It feels OK. I guess maybe I did get kind of begging last night didn't I? I had never been fucked before, and for as long as I had been wanting it, once I got a chance, I was way too anxious for it again and again! Shit man, I'm glad I was with three guys for my first time. I'm afraid that if I had been with only one guy, he might not have been able to keep doing me like I kept begging for last night. Guys – all of you – man I have to thank all of you for what you did for me last night! You really made me know who I really am! I really do have to thank you guys a lot. I always wondered about getting it up the ass, but until last night, I was just too damn afraid to do it. You know men, last night you three guys really helped me figure me out, a lot!"

"Well, I guess you are welcome!" Jake said. "I'm not too sure we were trying to help you figure anything out, but if we did, then I guess I'm glad we were there. Are you kind of trying to tell us that you know for sure now that you are gay, and not the straight guy that you have been trying to be?"

"Yes! That is exactly what I am trying to say. I have wondered for a long time now if I was really straight and just playing around once in awhile with guys, or was I really gay and playing around once in awhile with girls. Now I know! Now I've got some crap that has to be taken care of, and try to get my life all put together again."

Jimmy looked at Michael and very seriously asked. "Michael, what are you saying? Are you saying that you are going to dump Sharon? Is that what you're saying?"

"Yeah man, that is what I am saying! She and I fight all of the time anyway, and now I know for sure of why we do that. Hey, today is going to be another one of those days! Screaming and hollering! Before I came over here last night, I did call her and tell her that I would be late, but at that time I did not realize that I would be staying all night. Yeah, a lot of the crap that is happening between us is my fault, and now is the time for me to start doing something about it. I'm going to move out! It took something like last night, and this morning for me to realize that I'm messing up my life and Sharon's too. It's over! Now, I just have to figure things out!"

"Jay," Jake said to his brother. "Why don't you and I go upstairs and use the upstairs bathroom to get ourselves kind of put together for the day, and Jimmy and Michael can use the one down here."

Then turning to Michael and Jimmy, Jake continued. "Guys, when you get ready, come on up and we'll get some breakfast, or maybe by this time it will be lunch, but anyway something to eat. Michael, I kind of think Jimmy has got a pretty good head on his shoulders, and if Jimmy doesn't mind, why don't you kind of tell Jimmy what you think you are going to be doing, so that you have somebody to bounce ideas off of. Is that OK with you Jimmy?"

Jimmy replied. "Yeah, it sure is! You guys go on up and Michael and I will be up as soon as we shower up a little and get dressed. You are right, this will give us some time to kind of talk about what Michael is about to go through – so that he has his mind on kind of straight. – Whoops! – Should not be using that word today, should I?"

Jay and Jake kind of gathered themselves together and went upstairs. Jimmy and Michael both headed for the basement bathroom since neither one of them had taken that morning piss that they each needed to take.

Michael was the first one to take a leak, and as he started, he turned to Jimmy and told him to step in the shower and turn the water on.

Jimmy replied, "Yeah – but I got to take a leak too!"

"You will!' Michael replied. "But you are going to take a leak all over me! You gave me some new experiences last night and you are going to continue today. You are going to give me your piss!"

"Shit man!" Jimmy said. "Shit man, you really are getting into this new stuff pretty fast now that you know you like it, aren't you?"

"Yeah, I figure I might as well go for just about everything that I've been thinking about for so long. Along with wondering just what it would be like to get a dick up my ass, I've wondered for a long time what it would be like to watch a guy dump all of his piss on my chest, and Jimmy, it is your piss that I am going to find out with."

"Well, Michael, stop pissing, then, man! Save some of that for spraying on me too, then! I didn't know we were going to be doing this!"

Michael immediately grabbed ahold of his dick and forced himself to stop pissing.

Jimmy got in the shower and turned the water on. Michael followed him in, still grabbing ahold of his cock, so that he would not be dumping any more 'man water.' He turned Jimmy around so that they were face to face and immediately started spraying Jimmy with the piss that he had left.

Jimmy reached out for Michael's piss and splashed it up higher onto his chest and splashed some of it up under his arm pits. "Man, that's warm piss!" Jimmy said, and then continued, "Michael, I have to admit to you that I have never had a man piss on me before. I've kind of thought about it, but just never had the right guy around to ask him to do it. You and I are kind of finding the same things are exciting to us, I guess! Aren't we?"

"Yeah, I guess but come on man! Start your flow man!" Michael pleaded. "Come on man, spray me! Piss on me man! Get me all pissed on! Hey – I've heard the term 'pissed on' many times before, but I don't think it was ever in this context. Yeah man! I want pissed on!"

Michael was rather quickly loosing the last of his piss and told Jimmy. "Shit man, if I had ever thought that you would be so agreeable to this pissing shit, I would have never used the toilet, I would have used you for my toilet, but I'm about all out of piss, so now it's your turn. Stand still man and get it going. I'm getting really anxious for it. Spray me good and strong!"

As Michael made his statement of, 'good and strong', he sat himself down on the floor between Jimmy's legs. He placed his head right in front of Jimmy's crotch. "Pee on me man! Pee on me!"

Jimmy was more than just a little surprised of Michael sitting down in front of him, but he had no problem with that new position.

He asked Michael, "You want it in the face, man? You want me to spray your face?"

"Yeah, Jimmy, yeah man. Pee in my face. I want to feel your piss dripping down my face!"

With that statement, Jimmy started his pissing! He knew and had been told what Michael wanted, and he will willing! "Michael, I've never pissed on another guy before! This is really getting me all turned on, man. I like doing this! Shit man, take my piss! Oh Michael I never thought I'd be doing this to anybody today. Shit man! I like this! Hey, Michael, can I spray your mouth?"

Michael answered by shaking his head, 'Yes.' He kept his mouth tightly closed, but he turned his head up toward Jimmy's flowing dick, and positioned his face so that the warm 'man water' was hitting him right in the face. Jimmy could hear Michael moan an exciting moan of pleasure. Michael kept moving his head so the stream would continue to hit different places on his face.

"Michael, baby." Jimmy said. "I'm running out of piss man. I want to keep you all wet all day long, but man I'm going dry!"

All of a sudden Michael shook his head 'no' and let out a 'no' sound. All of a sudden Michael opened his mouth and immediately aimed his open mouth for Jimmy's flowing cock and sank his mouth on the cock and the flow, as quickly as he could. Jimmy was completely shocked. Michael had been keeping his mouth so tightly closed, that Jimmy was sure Michael did not want to taste the piss, just feel it. All of a sudden, things changed!

Jimmy stood there, continuing to empty his bladder and realizing that Michael was drinking everything that he had left. As he felt like he had gone dry, Jimmy squeezed his body so that any piss still left inside of him would be forced out and into Michael's mouth!

As Jimmy drained the last of his water, Michael pulled his mouth off of Jimmy's dick and immediately threw it up against Jimmy's crotch and grabbed ahold of Jimmy's butt, and hugged him as tightly as he could. Michael took a very deep breath!

Jimmy was very sensitive to what Michael was experiencing right then. In his comfort and caring, Jimmy wrapped his arms around Michael's head and told him, "That's OK baby. Everything is OK! Sit there a moment and just let me hug your head. You are OK, baby, you are OK!"

Jimmy knew that Michael was mentally tripping. He knew that when he had opened his mouth and started drinking the piss, that was an action that he never thought out. His inner wishes and desires had completely overtaken his mental process, and although he was constantly telling himself to keep his mouth closed, his stronger inner powers took over, and now he was shaking with fear and with some embarrassment of what he had done. He had just fulfilled a fantasy that he mentally thought he would never be able to do. All of his upbringing and all of his earlier teachings had told him that to do something so personal and so closely connected to another person, especially a man, was just something to never be done. He had done it! He was waiting, mentally, for the earth to come to an end. He had done what no man was ever to do, and although it was the most of terrible things for a man to even think about even wanting to ever do, he did it, and he was glad! He took another big deep breath.

"Oh Jimmy! Oh Jimmy, I drank some of your piss, man! I did not know I was going to do that! I thought I was just going to have you spill your piss on my head. Jimmy, I did not plan that. All of a sudden I had my mouth open and I had your dick and your piss in my mouth. Jimmy, I had to swallow it man! My mouth was full of your cock and I kept pulling it in farther. I had to swallow it or I would have gagged! Oh Jimmy! Shit man! Is that OK with you that I did that"?

"Michael, why in the hell wouldn't it be OK with me! Shit man! That was hot! Michael, I have wondered what it would be like to piss in a guy's mouth for a long time, but never had anybody that I could do that to. Michael my baby! You have really given me some really high excitements by doing that! Oh Michael, I would have never had the nerve to ask you to drink it from me, but oh man, I am so damn glad that you did! Michael, you are a real man! You have guts man! Thank you for drinking from me! I will always remember this!"

The two new friends – new friends that have now experienced more new adventures together faster than most friends do over a much longer period of time – washed each other completely and rinsed each other's bodies. After finding a couple of towels to use, they dried each other off, gave each other a big sized bear hug and headed back into the playroom where their cloths were. As they dressed, they discussed what they thought Michael's next move should be in regards to Sharon, and that mess. Jimmy assured Michael that if he found out that he was the one that had to get out, that he did have room for him at his apartment, and that he was welcome to it, until things could be figured out on a little more patient basis.

"Thank you man!" Michael emphatically told Jimmy. "Really man, I have to admit that for months now, whenever I thought about the idea of telling Sharon that it was over between us, it was the scare of where can I go if I have to leave, instead of her packing and going. Jimmy, I really do appreciate it! Can I really stay with you for a week or two, if I have to get out?"

"Yes, Michael, you can. I would not have told you that unless I meant it! You have some nasty times coming up, and you need to know you have some friends around you so that you can do what you need to do. OK, man?"

Michael gave Jimmy a big hug and thanked him again.

The two finished getting themselves dressed and went upstairs to join Jay and Jake.

"Hey guys!" Jake said as the two came into the kitchen. "Jay's on the phone in the living room. Somebody called, but I don't know who it is. Probably another one of his secret tricks! I'm sure he will be out here shortly! So did you two get all showered? – Oh shit man! Hey, did you guys find towels to use? I completely forgot to get some out for you."

"Yeah, we did." Jimmy said. I guess any we found down there were OK to use, or they would not be down there, right?"

"Yeah." Jake replied. "Anything you found is OK. Did you guys get a chance to hash out what Michael needs to be doing now and how he's going to handle things?"

"Yes, we did." Jimmy told Jake. "He has decided that when he gets home today, if she is there, he is going to tell her that it's over. I told him that he can stay with me for awhile if he is the one that is forced to get out. From what he has told me, and together with what he did last night and this morning also, I kinda think he realizes that the time has come for him to live his own life."

"Uhh – What he did last night, and this morning also? I didn't see him do anything this morning!" Jake firmly stated. "Uhh, what do you mean by 'this morning?' What did I miss? I guess something was happening before you guys woke us up, since nothing much happened after we got up!"

Jimmy looked at Michael and kind of made a funny face like – oops – I goofed!"

Michael looked at him and with kind of an embarrassed look on his face, and said. "That's OK Jimmy. Tell him. Unless you don't want him to know – it's OK with me."

Jake looked at both men and said, "So, tell me what, men? What did I miss out on here?"

Jimmy told Jake about the 'watering' events in the shower earlier.

"Shit man!" Jake exclaimed. Looking at Jimmy, he continued in a very excited manner. "You pissed in his mouth, and you did it in my house, and I got left out!? Damn man! I have not pissed in any guy's mouth-well, except for 'ole toilet bowl Jay' – for so damn long – and I have been wanting to find me a mouth and I have one here in the house and I get left out? Damn man!"

Jake grabbed Michael and gave him a good one armed hug and said, "Well man! I am really proud of you for that, and as soon as I can get my bladder good and full again, I just hope that you will take some ole piss from a big black dick as happily as you did from that ole pale white dick."

"Wait, wait men!" Jimmy interrupted. "Wait one damn minute here men. Just because I was the faucet this morning, that's only because I did not know early enough of what was going to be happening. If you guys are going to be giving each other warm pee drinks, don't plan on leaving me out! Yeah, compared to you two 'more experienced guys' I've never drank a guys piss before, but I guess maybe it's time for me to get some new experiences too, so don't forget me when the water starts flowing!"

"OK man! We'll make sure everybody is there and nobody is left out! This idea will really get Jay all excited. He has not been in a piss fest – well as far as I know of, anyway – for a long time. He's the kind of guy that likes to get piss from about three guys all at the same time so that he can mix it up in his mouth before he swallows it! He is truly a piss hound."

"Who's a piss hound?" Jay asked as he came into the kitchen.

Jake, Jimmy and Michael filled Jay in on the conversation that he had just missed while on the phone.

Although Jay did express some happiness over the idea of a future piss fest, he did not act or sound very happy or excited as the other three men were.

Jake looked at him and asked. "Hey, Bro. You're not acting so – up, all of a sudden. Everything OK? Who was that on the phone? Is everything OK?"

Jay grabbed a glass of juice off of the counter and said. "Well man, I really don't know! That was Patrick on the phone. He's going to be over here very shortly. He and his lady broke off the marriage last night. He realized that marriage was the wrong thing for him, and after all the shit that happened last night, he tried to find me so that he could talk, but we never heard the phone, and when he drove by the house he saw extra cars here, but didn't see anybody through the windows, so he didn't know where I was. I'm feeling bad since he needed me as a friend and I wasn't there for him. Anyway he's coming over, and I told him that you know about our playing around together and he's glad I told you. I told him that Jimmy and Michael are here, and he said that right now he just needs some friends around him, so if it was OK with you guys, he wanted to come spend some time with us. That's OK I hope?"

"Well, of course it's OK Jay! I'm sorry we weren't available for him last night too. Shit man. We could have had another one down in the basement to play with. But, of course, I'm not too sure he might have been in the mood for playing, with what he had already gone through. This is turning out to be quite a day isn't it? First Michael and Sharon, and now Patrick and his lady!"

Then looking at Jimmy, Jake asked. "Oh hey – Mr. Jimmy! Are there any secret women in your life that we just have not heard about yet?"

"No, no man!" Jimmy replied. And up until yesterday, I really didn't have too many men in my life either, but shit man, what a change of events can happen all of a sudden! You three guys, and now I'll get to meet this Patrick guy, too! Four new friends all within one day! Now that's pretty good going, I'd say!"

Chapter 9

It feels like I am fucking myself!

"Jay, I still don't fully understand everything from last Sunday!"

"Like what Jake, what do you mean?"

"Well, the way Michael and Patrick took to each other so fucking fast. For two guys that really were facing some shitty days ahead of them, they sure didn't act like there were any problems."

"Yeah, yeah you are right! You know, I think part of it might have been the fact that neither one of those two were very experienced in the playing around arena, and maybe you and me and Jimmy were just a little too much for them, and they felt better with each other. What do you think?"

"You know, I kinda think maybe your are right! After Patrick got here – I can't believe it! Really, did you notice how those two guys started hitting it off with each other? That Patrick and Michael were acting like long lost friends that just found each other again."

"Oh yeah Jake, oh yeah! I noticed!"

"When Patrick came in, I expected him to be all pissy and down in the mouth from what happened the night before that – the breaking up the marriage and stuff, but hey – just sitting here at the table I kept watching him and Michael looking back and forth at each other, and I was wondering then if they were gonna jump each other just sitting here at the table. You know Jay, when he came in, you were really the only person here that he really knew – well, yeah he knew who I was but, not like he knows you, and of course, you sitting there all bare assed naked and that rod of yours sticking out like some bamboo bush, it did take him a minute or two to kinda feel like he fit into the group. But man alive, all of a sudden he started paying attention to every little word that Michael said! Hell man, he even kinda quit trying, to keep looking over at your dick some."

"Yeah, you know what Jake? I noticed that he really started paying a lot of attention to Michael after Michael started talking about some of the stuff that he got into the night before. I know you noticed too, how a little later he asked Michael if he'd take him down and show him the playroom, since he'd never seen it."

Jay and Jake were discussing the elements of the previous Sunday, and the events that had happened since Patrick had come to the house, and also discussing some of their additional activities with Jimmy, as Michael and Patrick had enjoyed themselves downstairs.

"Did you notice how Patrick just seemed to be awestruck with everything that Michael said or did? Man, once he kinda just got to know him, he was like all over him!"

"Yeah, I know." Replied Jay. "When I and Michael took him downstairs to show him the playroom, it only took Patrick about one second to get to him and let him know he was real anxious to get in his pants! And, to top it off, I was the one standing there with my dick hanging out, and this time, he didn't pay one bit of attention to it. I was standing there, all dick out and ready to use it, on either one of those two, and all of a sudden I was just kind of like ignored."

"Well what happened? I figured you were gonna stay down there and play around some, but what happened?"

"That Patrick, he just all of a sudden took off like he'd been doing the guy thing for years! He had his hands all over Michael, and of course Michael didn't resist any! He just stood there and let Patrick strip him totally!"

"So I guess just letting those two stay down there all by themselves must have been the right thing to do, then right?"

"Yeah, I guess so! Everything must have gone pretty good for 'em. Like I told you earlier, Patrick called earlier and told me that since he and his gal broke up, he and Michael have really been spending a lot of time together. Sharon threw Michael out since he didn't come home that day until about five or six at night, and I guess he kinda already had it set up with Patrick that if that happened, he was to go over to Patrick's place. So, from what I gather from what he said today, he and Michael are now living at Patrick's."

"Shit man, I can not believe how fucking fast things changed for those two guys last week-end. I mean, Jimmy had told Michael that if things got bad at his place, he could go stay with him at his place, but then all of a sudden, he's staying with Patrick."

"I know it, but I gotta be honest man, I'm not too up-set with any of it, are you?"

"You know Jay, I'm real glad they ended up the way they did. I gotta be honest man and tell you that I really do think both of us are too big for either one of those guys, body wise and dick wise! Jay, we are big guys, and neither one of those two are really very big guys! Let's face it man, our getting Jimmy is definitely the better to the deal. Now that man, he plays and he knows how to play!"

"Shit man, I'd say so too! When I came up from the basement last Sunday, you and Jimmy shocked the shit out of me with you having him on the kitchen floor and fucking the hell out of him. Just how in the hell did that all get started, I mean man, I'm not sorry it did, cause I got some rocks shot off that day too – but just what in the hell happened that got that all started?"

"We were sitting at the table, just kinda finishing up our breakfast or whatever it was at that time, and he picked up one of his sausage sticks, looked at it, really gave it a very desired look of love, licked his lips, looked over at me and said, 'Oh how I like 'em dark brown, stiff, hard, long and thick, and oh so sweet in my mouth!' He looked at me, and then started sucking on the sausage, and rolling his lips around on it. Shit man, I will admit – the way he was lusting all over that little sausage stick and licking on it and kinda making love to it – hell yes man – that got me all turned on! Just watching him looking at that little sausage stick made me know he was wanting my dick in his mouth again, and all of a sudden, he sucked that sausage stick down into his throat in one big gulp, swallowed it whole, I guess, and then all of a sudden he was down between my knees, had my shorts pulled off as far as he could get 'em to go, and let my sausage stick follow the other sausage stick. And I swear, in one big gulp! That man can swallow dick! And Jay, we're both carrying pretty big sticks, and our Jimmy guy does not have any problem taking either one of 'em. I still think we found ourselves a pretty good toy! I do!"

"Hey brother – I agree – I do! Last Sunday when I came up from the basement – yeah – I will admit, I was pretty well bummed out since I realized that the two in the basement were more interested in each other, and not me! I gotta admit it man, hardly ever – and I mean ever, does some guy get all excited over some other guy when I'm there, and especially when I'm standing there totally naked, showing everything I've got, and making sure anybody standing there right then, can have whatever they want! Jake, seriously man, I don't ever remember that happening to me before. Yeah, I will admit that there have been some times when later, I kind of wished I had not offered my meat to someone, but hey – at least they wanted it and did not turn away from me! So when I got upstairs and found you two beating the hell out of each other's asses, I was fucking glad!"

"Well, I know one thing man!"

"What, what's that?"

"Whatever happened or did not happen in the basement while you were down there, sure did get you going once you were up stairs! I'm laying there fucking the hell out of Jimmy and that tight sweet ass of his, and all of a sudden, while I'm fucking Jimmy, I'm now getting fucked by you! Jay, it's been quite a while since one of us fucked the other one while he was in the process of making a family man out of some other guy, but let me tell you – I liked it! Yes, I did! All of a sudden realizing that my big, hung, stud of a brother, was now in the process of poking my butt while I'm poking Jimmy – that was hot! Fucking hot! I liked that, and I need to tell you that I did! I really did! Everything last Sunday got all kind of busy and confused, and I never told you that I was glad you did that, and hell man – I guess you already know how Jimmy liked it! When he tried to look back and see just what was happening, when he found out that you were up on me, and he was then really kinda of getting fucked by both of us at the same time, I thought he was gonna go wild!"

"Hey Bro, I'm glad you liked it! Yeah, it's been too long since we did a double stack Big Mac type of thing. I'm glad it worked out the way it did! Like I said – I got some rocks off that day too, and I'm still not sure of just what Jimmy meant when he was begging for, "God leave 'em in me man, leave 'em in me!""

"Oh, I kinda asked him about that later, and he had to admit that he did not remember saying it. He told me that he thought maybe, because any time that he has your dick, or my dick, up inside of him, it feels so good he knows he wants it to stay there forever and never come out, so he thought maybe that was what he was thinking about, but did not know he said it out loud!"

"I know he sure does like either on of 'em up in him, doesn't he?"

"Yeah, he does!" Jake answered. "Hey Bro, got a question for you. Like last Sunday, while you were fucking me, what does it feel like to you when you fuck me? What does that feel like?"

"It feels like I am fucking myself! Yeah, it does! Jake, when I'm on your back or got your legs up in the air and my dick stuck up in you, I feel like I'm fucking myself cause we are so much alike. Our bodies are almost identical, our skin is the same color, and I guess, when I'm in you fucking the hell out of you, I just feel like I'm doing me! Weird I know, but that's how I feel!"

"No, no it's not weird. That is exactly why I asked you! When I fuck you, there have been times when I actually closed my eyes, and mentally I felt my ass getting the action in it that I was really giving to your ass! Suppose we feel that way cause we're identical twins? If we were just brothers, and not identical twins, think we'd feel that way?"

"Hell, how in the hell am I supposed to know! I just know it's fun to fuck you cause then I feel like I'm getting it in the butt too. But hey – Jake, I gotta find out yet! Last Sunday when we fucked on the kitchen floor, how in the hell did you two end up there? You told me that all of a sudden Jimmy was between your knees and was sucking on you, but how in the hell did you two end up on the floor? Especially in the kitchen?"

"Hey man, all I can tell you is, I was sitting there, Jimmy was down on the floor sucking like he'd not had enough to eat, and all of a sudden he pulled off, stuck his head out from under the table, and said, 'Hey man, I gotta get fucked again, I gotta! Please man, stick it up in me please! Please!' I got up and said, 'OK come on let's go to the bedroom,' and he said, 'No! No, I wanna do it here! I wanna get fucked here in the kitchen' – and so we did! And that's what was up, when you came up from the basement!"

"Well, let me tell you! That in itself was a fucking turn on to me! I do not remember any other time that we fucked on the kitchen floor! That was fun. And when we did the flipperoo, and I ended up on the floor with my gut laying there on the tile, that was another hot time. And let me tell you, when Jimmy ended up being the middle guy, with him fucking me, and you fucking him, all at the same time, that totally turned him on, and I mean a lot! Even with you up on top of him, and then him in me, when he shot off, I thought I was getting it from both of you two all at once."

"What time was it by the time we finally got all done in the bedroom? I know we got up from the kitchen floor, 'playground,' went in and took a quick shower each, since all three of us had cum all over ourselves, and then started all over again in the bed. Michael and Patrick must have stayed in the basement that entire time, right?"

"Yeah, I guess so! I know when they finally did come up, they found us in the bedroom and told us about how they found the leather stuff and how they blindfolded each other and did some stuff to each other that they never thought they'd ever be doing. Michael chained Patrick to the ceiling – remember him telling us about that?"

"Yeah and then Patrick strapped Michael down on the bench and first finger fucked him, then did a real fuck! I'm serious man, I really do think that day was almost the first really great time, for either one of those two. I think they are a natural fit for each other! I'm glad we had some part in getting them together!"

"You know Jay. For two guys that claim they've hardly ever done anything, like that, they sure are catching on fast!"

"You know, once in awhile it just takes two of the right guys, finding each other. I've been playing around with Patrick for what almost a year now, and he never did really take to it like he did with Michael. I really do think that he just needed a smaller man, and maybe one with a little less dick than me, but he never had the chance to meet anybody, and so he took up his best efforts by meeting me outside. You know, I kinda think those guys that try to hide across the road just might be like Patrick or even Michael. They just need to meet someone that they can relate to and then go from there. You remember how rough it was for even you and I to get something started between us, and hell man, we're brothers and we lived together, so you can imagine what it's like for the boys across the street or even Patrick and Michael."

Looking up from the table, and down the hallway, Jake made a remark. "Well look who is up! Good morning man! Kinda late getting up aren't you?"

Jay turned and looked, and commented, "Hey Jimmy my man! Time to get it up and going! Jake and I have already showered together, soaped each other up and cleaned out all of the little cracks and crevasses, made sure all of our body parts were still able to get stiff and strong, and of course still able to shoot off some early morning juices – had our breakfast, and were wondering just how long you intended to sleep in. We were just about ready to come in and fuck you awake. Not fucking wake you up, but really fuck you awake! Get your butt up in the air and fuck it till we knew you were really awake! If keeping you up till about two o'clock each night – so we can fuck the hell out of you and let you fuck the hell out of us, is gonna be too rough on you, then I guess we'll just have to cut back on the playtime! Good morning!"

Jimmy sat down at the table, Jake handed him a glass of orange juice, and said, "Don't let him bother you any man! That's just the way he is! He's a big brick, whichever end you are looking at! Jimmy, we are so fucking glad you agreed to come live here with us. We've been looking for a good guy like you for way too long now, and when we finally found you – and also found out just what you can do, are willing to do, and willing to try down in the playroom, we found ourselves a rock of gold! You are one fucking player man – you do it like we like it, and we're gonna take advantage of that and make fun for all three of us! You are one hot stud man, you are!"

Looking across the table to both Jay and Jake, Jimmy replied, "Men, don't thank me – let me thank you! Never in my wildest dreams did I ever think that I would ever get to play with a man like either one of you, and now I get to play with either one of you – whenever I want – or the better part is, living all together and I get to be the Oreo Cream in between the two hottest chocolate cookies, if there ever were two! A week ago, I did not even know there were two of you, and now I'm the luckiest and best fucked guy on this side of the world!

Never did I ever think that after my move a few weeks ago, I'd be moving again, but thank goodness, since they let me out of my rental agreement, I'm living the life of glory now, with two of the greatest men that any person could hope to have as friends, let alone everyday playmates. Jake, while you're out of town – now there's gonna be another guy here keeping track of your brother Jay, and making sure he ain't running around all naked and bare assed outside. But hey – if he is – it's probably because I'm right behind him and trying to catch him and maybe throw him down, right there in the yard! Men, I can't believe everything that has happened in just the past few days! About the only way that I can think to let both of you guys know how grateful I am about you wanting me to live here with you – is to make a pledge to you!"

As Jimmy raised his right hand and held it up high, he continued – "And that pledge is; 'To you Mr. Jake and to you Mr. Jay, I – Jimmy Stempff, do pledge, that for every time that you tell me that you wanna fuck me, and my ass, I will make my ass available – and I will let you do it twice! I also do pledge, that each time one of you gentlemen fuck me, I will just have to make myself, and my asshole available, to the other one, and let him fuck me too! I know, it's gonna be awfully, awfully, rough for me to do, but I gotta do something to let you know how thankful I am! Let me say – I guess it's the, 'price I have to pay!' How else can I let you know how thankful I am that I met you? Yes, I guess it's called doing double duty, but I really don't think I will be doing any big bitching about doing it at all! Thanks men – one hell of a big, big – thanks!"

About the Author

Wade Wright

Wade Wright is an older gay semi-retired gentleman who lives in Arizona, alone, except for his puppy of about 15 years. One "normal" marriage, two daughters, four grandchildren, and two sadly shortened gay partnerships, have given Wade a perspective of living very different types of lives, and uses some of those experiences, as he does his writings.

Wade Wright is also the author of:

- *Apartment 117*
- *Yes, Cops Do It – Oh Yeah*
- *The Two Straight Guys*
- *Marshmallow Cream – and Hard Big Pieces of Chocolate*
- *In Cemetery Park*

All available from Amazon.com,
The NazcaPlainsCorp.com, or your local bookstore.

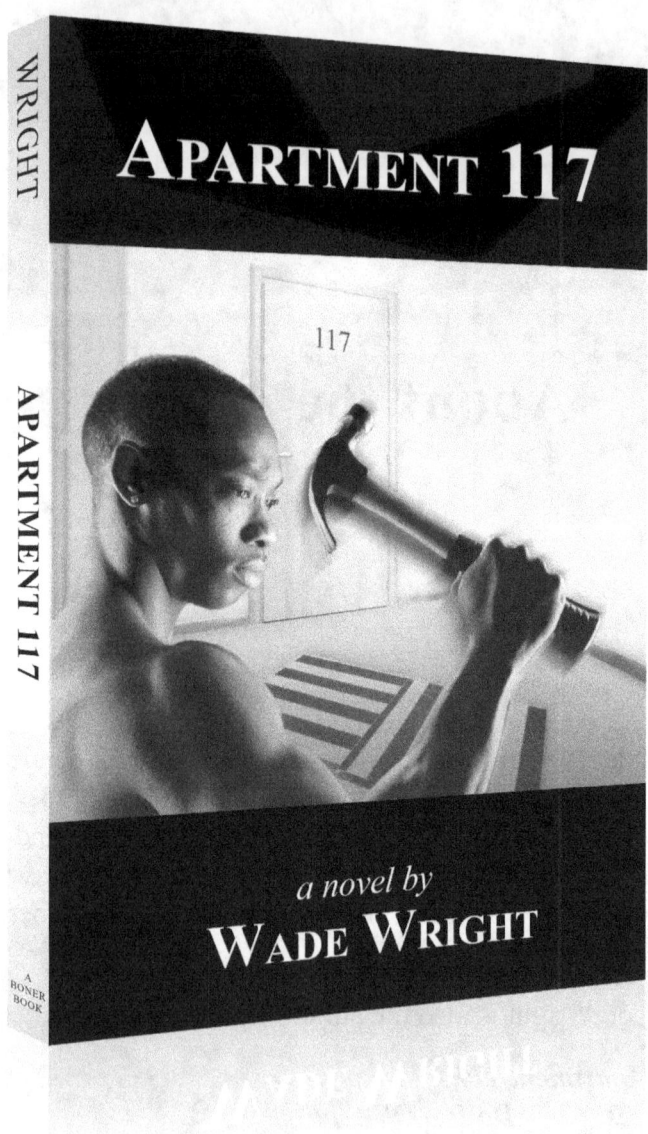

APARTMENT 117

117

a novel by
WADE WRIGHT

A
BONER
BOOK

WRIGHT

APARTMENT 117

MARSHMALLOW CREAM
– AND HARD BIG PIECES OF CHOCOLATE

EROTICA BY WADE WRIGHT

WRIGHT

MARSHMALLOW CREAM – AND HARD BIG PIECES OF CHOCOLATE

A
BONER
BOOK

The Two
Straight
Guys

a novel by

Wade Wright

A
BONER
BOOK

"YES, COPS DO IT, – OH YEAH!"

WRIGHT

"YES, COPS DO IT, – OH YEAH!"

a collection of stories by

WADE WRIGHT

A
BONER
BOOK

IN CEMETERY PARK

A NOVEL BY

WADE WRIGHT

WRIGHT

IN CEMETERY PARK

A DONER BOOK